C000175156

Published in Great Britain by
L.R. Price Publications Ltd, 2021
27 Old Gloucester Street,
London, WC1N 3AX
www.lrpricepublications.com

ISBN-13: 9781916887442

Dedication

For Beryl.

HOSPITAL SPIRITS

Paul Fields

I

Time to Go

1994

Ted felt heavy-hearted. That time to go to work was rapidly approaching again.

"Oh, bugger! It's half past six already, Tinkles," he said to his wife, Lucy.

Lucy sat curled up on the sofa, already in her P.J.s. "I know," she sighed, as her hazel eyes continued to read the newspaper, though moving very little. At that moment, she was more staring at the print than reading it, hoping to give the impression that she wasn't too disappointed that Ted would be gone in forty-five minutes. She vindicated the guise verbally; "Well, at least we've had most of today together, and we can do something nice tomorrow, before you go to work... again!"

They had enjoyed an Indian takeaway treat to soften the blow of Ted's return to work, even though they weren't exactly ships passing in the night, Ted only doing three twelve-hour night duties each week. Lucy herself worked Monday to Friday, in flexible nine to three or nine to five, depending on what the university's auditing department had lined up for her. Still, there was some strain on the couple; only married a year ago, they had hardly spent a night apart in the three years before Ted had taken this night-work position.

Lucy didn't ask how many shifts Ted was doing this time. He didn't have the heart to tell her it was Saturday to Tuesday; a back-to-back work rota – oh, joy! *When she asks, I'll break the news,* he thought.

"Let's just watch half of *Cook Spoofs* before you have to go in the shower, shall we?" suggested Lucy, with her great persuasive appeal.

"We can watch it up to the first break," Ted agreed, readily, "then you can tell me about the second half once I'm ready. I wonder who they will be taking the piss out of tonight."

Lucy leapt at the opportunity to give Ted a preview, having seen a trailer for the show that morning. "They are doing a character called 'Papa Tagliatelle' tonight," she giggled, as she stretched and yawned, then continued: "it looks like it's poor Italy's turn to be targeted this week."

"Italian food is great! They must be putting a different slant on the show this week," Ted reasoned.

"Yeah," Lucy agreed, "it's easy to make fun of Polish dumplings or Middle Eastern 'soup that can see you'."

Ted laughed. "Or the Russian stew made in a cement mixer

– without bothering to take the cement out first – used to make cannonballs for the latest 1812 costume drama! Ha-ha-ha, they lost more extras to this cook's 'safe' cannonballs than the Russians lost in the real Battle of Borodino." His broad shoulders shook in further laughter.

"Oh, yes, that would particularly appeal to your geeky history head. I'm surprised you didn't wear a Napoleon costume to watch the show!"

Before Ted had the chance to whip up a witty riposte to his wife's playful mockery, she cut in again, as the show was about to start. "Well, here goes," declared an amused, mischievous-looking Lucy.

They enjoyed twenty minutes of slapstick and parody, as a top Roman restaurant was transformed into a spaghetti, pasta and pizza dough frenzy of food-fighting groups of guests. This all happened because a well-meaning Papa Tagliatelle had decided to save money, by starting to cook and serve the food himself.

"Well," Ted sighed, "I'd better go and get ready for work now. It hasn't been as good as the last three shows – still funny, though."

"It's okay. I hope they aren't drying up on ideas. I love this show," lamented Lucy. "I'll let you know how it ends, sweetie."

Ted massaged her slender shoulder for a few seconds, then went upstairs to enjoy a hot, refreshing shower. He was washed, shaved and dressed in fifteen minutes.

As he traversed the stairs, Ted asked Lucy how the show had panned out.

"There were a few more minutes of slapstick, then when Papa started presenting the bills to the diners, they chased him down the street in a large, angry mob! He managed to commandeer a scooter, but a few of the mob did, too. He rode on to the Circus Maximus, while it played *Gladiator*-style music. Then, one of his pursuers knocked him off the scooter with a lethal chunk of pizza base, while he was distracted by a Roman soldier charging toward him with a two-donkey chariot, at comedy high speed. The last scene showed him washing up a huge pile of dishes in someone else's restaurant."

"Hmm, not the greatest show, then. Let's hope next week is funnier," said Ted.

"Not likely," said Lucy; "I noticed on the end credits that it's an international production, so the style of humour might vary a lot. We can watch the next one properly, maybe?"

"Definitely; I'm off then," smiled Ted.

"Hoorah!" Lucy shouted, partly in mock jubilation.

"Okay, darling, see ya in the morning. Love you," Ted sighed.

"Love you too, Bear. See ya soon." Her eyes again took refuge in the direction of the day's newspaper.

Ted glanced back from the porch door. Her hazel eyes had raised slightly above the newspaper, deep and very brown, in the play of light and mood.

Three other deep brown, doleful sets of eyes also fixed on him, adding to his guilt at departing and abandoning them. His head slowly moved to the relevant points of the sitting room, blowing four corresponding kisses to the girls he loved.

"Have a great girlies' night in. Byeeeee!"

Further salt was rubbed into Ted's wounds as he motored through his beloved village. Leaving Cilchester behind for any but the most exciting of outings was always a difficult feat – but when going to work... ugh!

Ted had taken night duty at a different hospital in order to get promoted to mid-grade staff nurse. It was an unpopular decision with his wife, but she understood the necessity career-wise. As he drove through the village, he thought back to his previous post, his first permanent position as a junior staff nurse. This new job had its stressful moments, but it was a breeze compared to the remorseless stress of a busy medical ward on day shift. He no longer felt that he was being torn in four directions at once, like some Roman execution before a voyeuristic, baying crowd of visitors, relatives, social workers and managers; now, only the occasional horse dragged a single rope-burnt limb at a time – at least, most of the time this was so.

My god, he realized, *that daft show is in my psyche! Alarm bells.*

He was working with a much nicer crew now; more support and less back-biting. He was more confident after two years of post-qualified experience. He was now under a charge nurse and amongst colleagues who, in the main, he felt comfortable working with.

As if to balance his mood with this contrived "feel-good" factor, it was 7:22 on an optimum summer evening, in late June. Bright mornings and time in the garden always boosted morale, as well as his natural suntan; Ted had olive skin which darkened quickly in the sun. He got a kick out of being asked where he had been on holiday, and replying that he had only been in the garden and walking his dogs.

While cruising along the dual carriageway, often above the instructed speed limit, comforting and familiar tones flowed from the car radio. *Yay! I've cheered myself up!* Ted gave himself a metaphorical pat on the back.

But, nearing the town centre – the only part of the journey that he objected to – now loomed. Three successive mini-tunnels served flyovers built to reduce traffic congestion. Ted wasn't convinced of their effectiveness, as he sat in a traffic jam underneath one of these tunnels.

The music from the radio crackled, became disjointed, then ceased altogether; his only entertainment now was a rear view of the racing green, two-seater sports roadster in front of him, in which a smartly kempt man in his sixties conversed with a very attractive brunette lady in her late twenties. *Nice cars have their perks,* he thought, then considered: *I may only drive an old, powerful saloon, but I have a wife more beautiful than that tidy lady.*

It was at times like this that Ted became aware of one of his nervous quirks: he would get a tune fixated in his head and make up silly lyrics to it, whether he knew the real words to the song or not. He inwardly cringed at his stupidity, as he heard the lyrics coming from his tone-deaf voice-box:

"Let's all master bake.

This is a tea cake!"

What the hell?

No, there was more:

"Let's all masticate,

to eat up our cheesecake…"

When he realized that he was repeating this in a cycle, it started to get on his nerves.

Mmm… he thought, *how about a ditty on Victorian moral*

values?

> *"Let's not masturbate;*
>
> *then we'll get a cream cake!"*

His inner psyche caused him embarrassment again. The problem was that, when under stress or very deep in thought, he sometimes did this in the street, the supermarket or, worst of all, at work, when he thought there was no one around. This was embarrassing for a man in his late twenties. *I must work on this Achilles heel,* he promised himself. It was just one of a few entries on his to-do list.

Now the concrete maze was at last left behind, and the tired white workhorse engaged her several equine power pistons, in order to ease a right through the large, late-Victorian entrance to the hospital. He found a suitable parking space for her in the makeshift car park.

Ted then resigned himself to four long nights of the same.

II

The Man in the T.V.

Ted punched in the security code to the main entrance. The numbers gave away the department manager's age; *Almost retirement time, you lucky woman!* He next signed the visitor book, including precise time, printed name, signature and car registration. Mischievous Ted was tempted to write his shoe size, but Responsible Ted restrained him, as so often happened. He often forgot to sign the book, and was subsequently reminded by the departmental matron (secretly known to most as "Hattie") that it would not do to have the fire brigade risking life and limb, searching for persons unidentified in the register. Once, as she told him the same old thing, he was tempted to reply that he would put nametags in all of his uniform items, so that if he was burnt to death, he would be identified should one of the nametags survive. But then, boring old Responsible Ted stepped in again, to keep him out of trouble.

"Oh, it's you on tonight, Ted?" Yolanda's large, round, brown eyes widened in genuine satisfaction, peppered by a touch of mild sarcasm.

"Yes, first of four," Ted sighed, secretly happy to be

working with the warm, experienced and reliable Yolanda.

On the occasional bad night, she may not speak to you for an hour or two. Then a truce would be heralded – only by her – when an opened bag of sweets appeared on the table, or you were offered a hot drink. Or, the highest honour, she invited you to look at her latest batch of photos. Ted always welcomed these truces, with great relief that this great ally had restored cordial relations. Some of the staff called her "Yol" or "Yolly", but Ted didn't yet feel that he should be crossing that line of familiarity – even after nine months.

In these early years, Ted wasn't a believer in checking and memorizing who he would be working with for the next week or two in advance. "Who else is on with us tonight, Yolanda?"

The ward's oracle replied with instant precision: "Debbie and Anna are on with you. I've got Claire, Zoe and Beth supporting me on fourteen. Zoe has a lot of ordering and other admin to do."

Ted's team all worked on ward 12A, named due to the founders' superstition, way back in the 1950s. Now the ward was approaching its own fifties, and the tradition had still stuck fast. Nurses and carers need all the luck they can get, so, for once, all agreed with management's decision: no ward 13 in this hospital. Patients' bed numbers, in all 56 wards of the huge hospital, were also designated 12A rather than 13. Lucky for some – not, unfortunately, for others!

Ted approached the men's changing room to put on his uniform. As he neared the door, deep in thought, he felt an agile form brush gently against his skin; a gliding, serpent-like presence wrapping around him. Then, he was aware of his right foot being pinned to the ground. A slightly irritating pain penetrated his light canvas plimsolls, from a sudden "friendly" gesture. Only slightly phased by all of this, on account of the irritating sensation in his foot, Ted looked down to see a white and steel-grey, striped beast wrapped around his ankle; Cleo looked up at him with contented, amber eyes. Between them was a tiny pink nose; long white whiskers extended far from the tiny face. He had seen that poise many times before. She looked up with a mixture of mischief and admiring recognition; Ted knew that, in her feline way of thinking, she was saying: "I'm sure you will like my latest cat joke."

"Here's my main gal," Ted jibed, as he picked Cleo up and hugged her.

Nine months earlier, as Ted had waited, with the usual healthy nervousness, to be interviewed for this post, a little nose and whiskers had peered cautiously around the corner of the L-shaped anteroom; she must have slinked through the slightly open window. Cat curiosity is quite unique. With the same slow, deliberate movements that the first feline queen to meet an ancient Egyptian grain-keeper must have made, at least five-thousand years ago, she prowled toward him, as he remained seated. It broke the tension of waiting, and Ted sniggered quietly at her antics. She glided against his smart, pin-striped, navy-blue trousers, in an offer of instant friendship. His polished shoes received a few designer cat-paw motifs, the dusty clay-grey contrasting nicely with the shining black, and Ted was worried that she would also cover his suit in hair, foiling any chances of employment here. But she didn't share the interviewee's concerns, and now confidently invited herself onto her new friend's knee, purring contentedly. She even gave her newfound friend the ultimate privilege of rubbing the scent of her recent, fish-flavoured lunch all over his trousers and shirt! *This is now an official friend of mine,* purred Cleo. After five minutes of mutual comfort, the dreaded office door creaked open, as the muffled conversation therein now became clearly audible, and Ted was ushered into the interview room by a friendly-faced executive.

"I see you have already met our top staff member," the man smiled.

Ted was relieved by the manager's cheerful disposition, as he feverishly brushed the fur from his suit, with limited success. He emerged forty-five minutes later with positive vibes about the course the interview had taken. The amusement of Mr. Sykes, the leader of the three panel members, had permeated proceedings; it brought a welcome undertone of informality to the professional and formal interview structure. Even Matron Jacobs (A.K.A. Hattie) had betrayed moments of slight amusement, behind the thick lenses of her large, oblong spectacles.

Four hours later, as Ted paced around the house, doing chores to keep himself busy, the phone rang. The new promotion was in the bag! Well done, Cleo!

Back in the present, once changed into his uniform, Ted smiled at Cleo with those happy memories, and went to listen to the handover report. It promised to be a quiet night for a change – that is, as far as medical pathology can promise quiet. Most of his patients were in a stable condition, and there were a lot of empty beds. This always seemed to happen on medical wards in the good weather; the cold winter months played havoc with our elderly people's health, while a beautiful summer seemed to benefit everyone. Happy days!

Ted paired up with Debbie for tonight's bed rounds. Having only nine patients out of a potential fifteen, on the acute wing of ward 12A, allowed them more time for therapeutic bantering, with the patients who were alert. By the next round, at about midnight, most patients would, hopefully, be settled, and "whisper mode" would be the rule.

"Are you still here, Sally?" Debbie's mischief bounced meanly off of Ted's well-meaning and calculated drollness, when they tried to cheer their patients.

"No," Sally sliced back, in a Londoner's lethal counter prose, "I've gone home to play tiddlywinks and bake some currant buns."

Ted knowingly escalated the contest: "Never mind that, Sally, we all know you're still here, because you haven't been paying your rent at home."

Sally's expression changed from carefree joviality to pure, immovable stone. "How dare you?!" she exclaimed.

Debbie and Ted looked at each other nervously. Had they overstepped the mark? Had they hit a raw nerve? There followed a good thirty seconds of working silence, as Sally's bed was tidied, and the bedside equipment and charts were checked. Then, Sally's stage mask lifted, compelled by the actions of the two silent workers in royal blue and butternut uniforms, and a welcome little hackneyed voice was again heard, from somewhere in the centre of the bed:

"I was going to pay the rent, then I looked in the newspaper and saw the wrecking ball knocking down number forty-seven."

Ted and Debbie stopped their official activities, looked at Sally, then at each other, and gave a laugh of relief. "What number do you live at?" Debbie ventured.

"Number forty-nine," said Sally, with her well-practiced solemn mask returning.

All three of them then burst into well-controlled laughter, knowing that Jen in the next bed was trying to sleep.

"Sally," Debs let her shoulders and head droop down in a gesture of mock dejection, "you are more than a match for both of us."

"Live and learn, Debs, live and learn."

The chastised two moved on. Temperatures, blood pressures, pulses and respiration rates were all checked by Debbie, and two concerns were reported by phone to the on-call houseman. Meanwhile, Ted brought out the medicine trolley.

After fifteen minutes, an observant, hard-working Debbie knowingly passed comment, as she passed Ted's trolley: "I bet a pound and a pinch of shit that Josh was on last night."

"That's an old expression," Ted marvelled. "Besides, his tell-tale signature is here, on all of the Medication Administration Records."

"Actually, I could tell," Debs stirred, "because you've been to the stock cupboard for a new box of empty meds at least four times, so far."

Ted sighed for effect, louder than was necessary. "There's

little that gets past you! Will you kick his arse for me, next time he's on with you?"

"Friday night." Debs was as in time to the beat regarding the off-duty rota as Yolanda was. "With pleasure, mate."

"Very kind, friend," Ted returned. So the exchange went on.

It was 22:41. All was quiet on both wards, with the exception of the swishing sound of life-giving oxygen, and the occasional delirious shout, deep sigh, cough or random statement. The junior staff from each ward took up post at the outstations. From there, they could closely observe the units farthest from the acute area in the centre. If any of their convalescents took a turn for the worse, they could quickly call for assistance where and when it was needed. The rest of the staff congregated in the central observation station, where the critical patients could be observed by the qualified and extended role staff, directly. With trained and tuned ear, they sat, listened and quietly conversed. There was no room in this inner sanctum for booming voices, after the night staff's imposed quiet time of 23:00; then it was sleep-therapy time for the patients. During these cherished quiet interludes, the staff mainly relaxed for a while, conversing, reading and daydreaming – at night.

The current topic was Claire's new photos. Claire had

recently moved house. Yolanda, true to form, was first to know when there was any news, the slightest work change, or general gossip to be investigated; therein was her special ability – her guile. Several gossip merchants frequented the wards; staff members, relatives, patients, social workers and doctors, in that order, could all be the ambassadors of hearsay within this confidential setting. Lots of information and gossip passed around the two wards, a high proportion of which was total crap. But some contained limited merit, and some was pretty credible. Yolanda deciphered it all.

At ward 14's outstation, Claire was feverishly catching up on care planning. Claire was a serious, conscientious workhorse – very much a "type A" person. She was working hard for her new family, her child and her partner, and she loved achievement through hard work. Her young partner was working hard in unison with her, and they were now proud of obtaining a mortgage for their new dream home. Now, a proud Claire was showing Yolanda, her mother figure, the first set of photos of her new home; Claire had moved to a new-build housing estate two weeks ago.

Yolanda, Ted's registered general nurse counterpart, was finally satisfied that "her people" – the acute patients of ward 14 – were all safe and sound, so she settled down, tentatively, to enjoy this latest visual update. Yolanda looked at each photograph with a big smile, as Debbie waited eagerly to have each passed to her next. It was great to see Claire doing so well; she had certainly earnt it.

Ted glanced over and smiled, also. *Must be a girl thing,* he chuckled inwardly to himself.

He got out his reading book, resolved to reading the same page several times if he had to. It wasn't easy to concentrate on a book at work; one ear listened down the critical wing, whilst the other paid mild, polite interest to the two ladies' reactions to the photos. Trying to achieve three things at once was hard work for Ted, and lapses of concentration on the book and the convo were frequent, especially in the closing hour of the night.

"Awww! There's her little boy! I think he's called Sammy," cooed Yolanda.

An eagerly waiting Debbie chipped in with her knowledge of something Yolly actually seemed unsure about: "She usually calls him Samuel, but now and then slips into calling him Sam, or even Sammy."

The photo showed Claire's little boy on his red baby tricycle – both baby and tricycle wore big, jolly smiles! He was in the front garden with Mum and Dad. The house was a pleasant, sand-brick, new-build semi, which appeared to have three bedrooms, with one built over the very spacious garage. A contrasting herringbone, sealed, red-brick driveway and hard stand area embellished a generous and well maintained open-plan lawn. Annual and perennial flower borders, and large potted displays, sold the scene.

As Yolly and Debs enthused about the house and garden, the garden's aspects made Ted's ears prick up, too. The three or four photos of the front of the house were followed by another four of the equally impressive back garden. Every angle of the garden was covered by these photos, sporting another good lawn and a decked area, which was obviously Samuel's main outdoor kingdom. It held a blue inflated paddling pool, adorned with Mickey, Minnie, Pluto, Donald and Goofy. Nearby, a car and garage playset had seen extensive action; there was even evidence of a couple of motorway pile-ups, here and there! Not to worry; a little fire engine and ambulance were at the scene!

As the photos were gradually passed from Yolanda to Debbie, they discussed Claire's family.

"They seem a very happy couple, don't they?" Debs exclaimed.

"They certainly do. I suspected Sammy would be a lucky little boy, by the way Claire is always proudly talking about him," smiled Yolanda.

"You can talk, Yolly!" Debbie and Yolanda had been close

friends since school, and in quiet, private times like this, Debs used her friend's informal address.

Ted had tried to remain detached from all of this, but he had reached an engaging part of his book and the end of a chapter. General Hood had accepted command of the army of Tennessee, and was about to lead his small assembly to near-destruction against Sherman's massive host. Ted decided to sit for a few minutes longer, secretly interested in his colleagues' gossip. He would soon check that the outstation staff were happy with their patients, and with their lot in general. It was a lot to hope for, he mused.

"Do you want to see these, Ted? It's a lovely house: one of those new builds on Johnstone Square."

How strange, Ted thought, within the capsule of his man-world, *I've just been reading about General Johnston trying to keep a Confederate army together! One of those strange coincidences.*

Yet, this phenomenon was chickenfeed compared to what the immediate future would behold for him – for what it would behold for all three present!

"I'll let you two look at them all properly first, then I'll have a quick scan later."

"Okay, Mr. American Civil War!" Yolanda teased him.

"More like Mr. Delighted-To-Be-Back-At-Work-After-Only

Two-Nights-Off!" Ted said, attempting to deflect the slight embarrassment which surged into him.

Female eyes rolled and glib smiles were given, then the girls continued to look at Claire's photos. The next shots moved inside the house. Yolanda studied each in detail, before ceremoniously handing them to Debs.

"Come on, Yols," Debs whined, "you are so nosey. Haven't you seen a house before?"

"Here you are, then..." Yolanda handed Debs the next offering in frustrating slow motion, just to wind her up further.

"Wow!" Debs exclaimed, as Yolanda's head sharply turned ninety degrees toward her, in quizzical alarm. "Here's a photo without Samuel in it!"

"Now, now!" Yolanda scolded her. "You've been doing too many shifts, Miss Grumpy. Miss Catty, even! Point noted, though." They both sniggered.

Two photos of a large, open-plan sitting room followed, then Samuel returned, this time playing with another toddler, also between two and three years old.

Yolanda's fair but frank eyes surveyed the main room of the house. "Nicely decorated, but I wouldn't have cream-painted walls and a cream carpet – at least until Sammy and any future little additions are a lot older!" Yolanda could get a little animated over things she felt strongly about. Her eyes widened and her mouth opened halfway; both hands went to her temples, then firmly clenched a strong, lacquered, black mane. She continued: "Those hands and feet may be small, but they are deadly to the decor! Phew! My Darren is my world, but one was enough for me, Debs."

"I bet you made the poor lad's life misery, following him around with dustpan and brush, detergent and spray. He was always escaping to his friends' houses, for days on end." She was going to take the wind-up further, but Ted was there, so it would be going too far. Instead, Deb's head went down at an angle, her eyes mischievously still fixed on her friend, to see her non-verbal reactions. Debs was the quieter of the two, and usually let Yol take the lead, but she had a little bite in her, too; she knew which buttons to press.

Yolanda's face remained deliberately calm, for full effect. A very challenging opponent, after thirty-nine years she was used to life's challenges. She had to repetitively tell patients things, day after day – sometimes more than daily.

She was from Athelport, born and bred. Most people could tell she was a local lass by her strong, clearly spoken accent. Her father was a northwest African sailor in the merchant navy, who had settled down with an Athelport-born girl, also of Moroccan descent, shortly after the war.

On an elderly acute medical ward, most of Yolanda's

patients would be aged seventy-plus. Oxygen masks and nebulizers were loud, confused patients sometimes shouted for long periods of time, very old people's memories were often short, and acutely ill people had pressing things on their mind, hence the inevitable question: "And, where do you come from, bonny lass?"

To which her repeatedly patient but forthright answer was: "Athelport, born and bred."

Now her calm expression remained, as she said to Debs: "Our Darren is fourteen now, and mainly does his own thing. As long as he digs in at school, and doesn't get into any bother, I believe in live and let live."

Debs's lower lip pouted slightly and her brow wrinkled. *Typical Yol,* she thought, *evading the question.* She decided to keep this as just a thought.

"Shall we get back to these last few photos?" Yol used an instructive tone, intended to place her back in full control of events.

"Awww! They are so cute!" Yolanda was suddenly beaming again. "I wonder if that other little boy is one of Claire's neighbours?"

"Probably," said Debs. "Mind you, she does have quite a few brothers and sisters; he could be a nephew, though I don't see any obvious family resemblance. We'll have to ask her later," she suggested.

Three similar scenes followed. In one, the two boys were playing happily in front of a large television, in Claire's sitting room. The T.V. was turned off. It stood on a wooden television cabinet, with glass doors and a mahogany finish. It was still the latter days of the videotape era, so a V.H.S. player was below the central part of the cabinet. Perched in front of the T.V., on the edge of the cabinet, were five neatly lined-up cuddly toys.

Yolanda's happy expression suddenly changed, as she flipped to the next picture. Her naturally large, round eyes widened further, as if they were about to pop out of her head. "Oohhh! I don't like the look of that!"

As Debs and Ted both quickly focused on Yolanda, she suddenly flicked to the next photo, in the hope that doing so would cancel out whatever she had just seen.

"Oh! I really, *really do not* like the look of that!! Oh, no!!"

Ted assumed that Yolanda was again being dramatic for effect. Debs, who had known Yolanda for almost thirty years, was more instantly intuitive. "Yolly?!" she exclaimed. "Oh, what is it, Yol?"

"I... I... don't really know... err... if I want you to see these next two photos." Yolanda's rich Arabic skin had taken on a very sudden ashen hue. Her eyes remained wide open in alarm, her mouth gaping and frozen. This very self-confident lady suddenly sat mesmerized, stripped in a second of her ability to act.

Debs reached over slowly, her small, now trembling hand flexed gently, fine fingers and thumb still closed against each other. Then, as the trembling limb delivered its hand very close to the pile of photographic worry, now abandoned on her friend's powder-blue lap, her first two fingers were ordered to open ranks, forming a scissor-like instrument which slotted in and selected the top three or four photos from a now dishevelled stack. The potentially toxic acquired load was retracted back to be dispensed on her own butternut lap, as the scissors melted away and a tense fist briefly replaced them. Concerned, pale-green eyes gazed down at the first picture.

Within a second her mouth suddenly jutted open – distressingly wide open – aping that of Yolly. The concerned, helpful eyes were awash with an involuntary tide of water, as sudden mental pain released its own defences! The second image showed her no mercy, doubling her pain. She suddenly felt warm dampness in her underwear, as a stabbing cramp grasped her bladder and groin. Yolanda hadn't even noticed that Debs had taken the photos.

Ted, however, still found himself firmly in the late-twentieth century, and he gawped at both of his colleagues.

What on Earth could be wrong with them? "Debbie...? Yolanda...? What's going on?"

For long seconds his enquiry seemed to bounce around in the space, which separated him from the stricken nurses.

"Oh, oh, bloody hell in shit!" Debbie uttered, finally allowed to relinquish her horrified paralysis, as Yolanda glanced vaguely toward the other two, still in silence, her eyes lost and now pleading for help.

"Take a look at these. They is really hobble... I mean... horrible," Debbie spluttered out her appeal to Ted. Her naturally pale skin was now almost milk-bottle white from shock. Debbie's right hand extended, quivering on the end of a semi-flaccid, sweating arm toward Ted's open and receptive large hand. To Debbie, this hand now seemed like the last refuge into which sanity and reassurance could be delivered. As he took the two photos from Debbie, her hand felt cold and clammy. Her legs crossed tightly and the foot pointing toward him began to rock rapidly up and down.

"Are you two okay?" he asked, bewildered.

"Of course not, numb-nuts! Look at them!"

Ted looked at Debbie without any anger, or desire to chastise her insult. With absolutely no idea what to expect, the staff nurse looked at the first offending image he held.

A deep chill instantly shot right through to his bones.

He saw the two boys laughing, as they pulled a favourite toy, tug-of-war style. Directly behind them was the mahogany T.V. cabinet, lined with soft toys, which must have been placed there by Mum or Dad. Behind the toys was a large T.V., which was obviously turned off because of its dull appearance. Yet, despite this, in the centre of the large screen, perhaps 48 inches, was an almost indescribable sight: an old man wearing a trilby leered out of the T.V., with the most evil expression in his eyes that Ted had ever seen, in all of his 29 years.

He gazed, transfixed in shock, as his colleagues had done. But, unlike the girls, who had quickly wanted to get away from the horror, Ted forced himself to study this awful image, in an attempt to make some sense of it; it had to be rationalized! Three years of debate with the super-realist Lucy had trained him to think like this.

But, despite his fear-filled resolve, after each few inquisitive seconds, Ted had to look away from this ghastly image. No matter how long he examined it, emotions with which he was familiar provided no acceptance of that face. It deepened nothing but feelings of fear, of dread, and almost an instantly injected concentration of depression.

He looked back at his colleagues. Debbie was looking slightly more composed now, but there was still evidence of discomfort. Deep sadness and concern had replaced her terror, in the almost two minutes since her initial shock. Her brow was shining with clear beads of sweat, running from her mid-blonde, tied back hairline. He also caught the still alarmed, wide eyes of Yolanda. She was composing herself a little, though the hint of a knowing expression invaded both of her irises and pupils, as if to say: *I understand how you feel, because of what you have just seen.* She was a very perceptive woman, even in times of great adversity. Maybe especially so at those times. The three of them now registered each other, but did not speak. Though Debbie's lips pursed to form a word, nothing was forthcoming.

Ted looked back at the first picture. A refresher did nothing to lessen the horrifying image. That evil head brought suppressive isolation into the very soul of a mere mortal; something therein sucked out life, value and hope – this even for the most positive and forward-looking of people. It made Ted feel like nothing – like shit!

Despite the instant feelings of negativity and non-achievement, Ted doggedly studied the photo in more detail. That T.V. was in no way turned on! *God...! A head with no neck and no torso, projected from a dull, turned off television screen. No, no... No way!* Ted shook his head, but coldness ran down his spine and overrode voluntary movement. Though his body became inert, his mind continued to work, yet with great effort. *There must be an explanation!*

Yet, part of Ted – his instinctive side, primaeval and dark – in fear of the unknown, also worked against his thought processes. The blackness soon started to win the contest.

The ageing man's head, complete with the old, slightly battered black trilby, sat in the middle of the lifeless screen. There was no neck and no shoulders. His looked like human features, but there was no humanity within that face! An oval presentation of negative, destructive power was introducing itself to our world, from another of black despair! A deep void filled Ted's soul.

Absorbed for what could have been hours by this nightmare image, Ted heard his own name entering this world of necrosis, drawing him back on a life-raft: "Ted...! Ted... Ted Tit-head!"

He suddenly looked up, to hear the voice transferred from his waking nightmare to the airwaves of the ward. "Ted!" This time it was being pronounced in tandem.

"Oh... what? Erm... sorry, ladies. This... really and truly... require some ports... All sports."

"Ted? What on Earth are you talking about?" Yolanda appealed to him for guidance, which wasn't forthcoming.

Yolanda, having taken the shock first, now drew on her strength of character, realizing and fully understanding the short-term plight of her friends. As the only readily available spokesperson, Yolanda had something important and devastating to tell Ted:

"Ted, please listen carefully, love. We have been trying to tell you that you are only looking at one of two pictures with that evil face."

"You what?!"

"There's another one."

Ted looked at Yolanda, still yet without further speech. His powers of analysis were gradually returning to him, but only, he felt, because the evil man in the T.V. was, at last, allowing it. But, why?

To Yolanda, Ted looked like someone who had already been exposed to too much, but she knew he was about to be subjected to even worse.

She projected her thoughts toward him: *Your fingers have been burned. You are still a novice, having yet to see all. Now you are at the point of putting your whole hand into the scalding bathwater and keeping it there.* She suddenly realized that her thoughts were very abstract and morbid.

Hang on, she realized, *I've had nasty thoughts as well. I think I am in shock! I've got to pull together now, to appear calm – no, to really be calm! A casual approach and normal behaviour might help all three of us now! Let me be calm; let me be normal,* she bargained with herself, in an inward stream of meditation. It worked for her partiality, as the image of that awful demonic face was diluted in her mind, interrupted by rippling interference from her determined mindset. *Cleanse it away... cleanse it away... cleanse... cleanse...*

For, Yolanda had a special gift. And, as her mind meditated, remedied and repaired, she helped to guide Ted through his trial.

"Come on then, Mr. Macho," she goaded the male nurse, the night leader, to face this new ordeal.

Ted stared at her for a while, then the first photo was slid behind the second; still he did not look down, appearing to carry out this simple task with the emotion of an automaton.

"Ted..." Yolanda suggested gently this time, appealing to him to look down at the photo. *I need all the emotional support I can get here,* she told herself. *We are all in this together now.* Finally, Ted gazed down at the second picture.

"Fucking hell!"

The ladies were startled and shocked afresh by Ted's use of profanity! Debbie and Yolanda both thought, along almost the same lines, that Ted hardly ever swore, and certainly not in the Anglo-Saxon vernacular.

All of the horror of the first photo was there, every bit as vile in presence as the first: the floating head; the red, diamond shape of those evil eyes; the cruel lips. All of these features were not human, just parasitically using a human guise.

But... no...

Oh, no!

In the first photo, those eyes looked straight ahead, straight at the poor victim who viewed the photo. In this second image, however, the eyes veered sideways, without any other discernible difference to the image, except for a slight, close-lipped smile which added sinister intent. Those inhuman eyes now looked directly at the two children.

This taboo phenomenon sickened Ted to his stomach; sudden sharp pain stabbed at his guts.

He looked straight up at Yolanda, who had stood up and moved closer to Ted for moral support. Their eyes fixed on each other, neither able to express the slightest reassurance; neither able even to blink, as long seconds passed. Ted saw thinly disguised terror, still deep within his colleague's densely pigmented irises. The pupils were small, but so deep as to almost merge with the surrounding circle of deep brown.

My god! he thought; the white borders to her slightly flickering eyes were now extensively bloodshot. Sudden intense strain had been too much for the tiny capillaries to withstand, and they had swollen in a bid to take over the normally pure white sclera. Yolanda was a hardened veteran of night duty, who almost always looked alert. But not so now.

And Yolanda saw in Ted's normally blue-grey eyes a sudden dullness. His pupils were still very large; the disproportionate discs gave a disturbing, doll-like appearance, almost of possession by something from outside of his soul. Or, could it be something from deep inside him? Something fleeing from this terror?

Eventually, someone spoke:

"Where's Debbie gone?" Ted's voice was flat, and there was no questioning intonation in his words. He felt them shake from his mouth, almost like corn flakes being scattered for birds, rather than into a cereal bowl.

"I think to the toilet, going by the look on her face after you saw the second photo!"

"What have we just seen?" Ted shook his head when he spoke, aware of perspiring droplets being distributed as he did so.

He noticed too the sweat on Yolanda's face. Her always perfect, prominent, black-lacquered hairstyle was now wildly sticking out in several directions. The armpits of her powder-blue uniform were darkened by large circles of moisture. She always had such an agreeable feminine aroma, probably topped up during heavy shifts, but for the first time there was an acrid smell of fresh sweat in the air; Ted soon realized that they both contributed to it equally. His own dark-blue tunic weighed on his back like a winter overcoat, the collar already wet and stale smelling. His uniform even had a damp streak down the centre, from chest to navel.

Yolanda looked at him for a while. Something must have been going on in that normally well-honed mind, yet Ted could tell that she was still struggling to make sense of it all – just as he was.

"I'm really, really worried. That is evil! I'm concerned for Claire and her little boy – and the other little boy, too." Her voice was resigned, similarly flat to that of Ted.

"I know that you are not easily upset by things like this. I know that you have had a few experiences of… 'supernatural' presence…" Ted rationalized.

"I have, but never anything as visual as this – or as terrifying. I can never look at those pictures again. Never! I know I can't, but I just want to destroy them both, to protect that family and maybe others. That's a demon in human form!"

Ted was still nullified, and didn't want to say too much, in case it came out as nonsense again. He thought, though.

Yolanda continued: "This is less spirit-related and more evil than anything paranormal I've ever experienced before."

Debbie returned, almost the colour of newly starched

hospital bedsheets. "I've been sick," she muttered.

Yolanda also knew of Deb's stress incontinence problem, since she'd had her two children – she would undoubtedly have been sorting herself out in that department, as well.

"Are you okay now?" Ted queried. Yolly didn't need to ask her friend; she always knew how she felt, instinctively.

Debbie replied: "Yes, it was just caused by the shock and feelings of upset."

After sitting and putting her head down, close to her knees, to give some relief to her stomach, Debbie arched her head upward once more, some rogue, untied curls of sandy locks obscuring much of her face. Her slender, red lips could still be seen, though; perhaps they could offer some hope, through speech?

III

Revelations and Remedies

"Claire can't have noticed that... 'thing' on those two photos; she was so proud, and happy about showing us them. That is really strange," Debbie declared.

"We aren't going to say anything to her!" Yolanda's assertiveness was returning now.

Debbie flung back her hair, stared at Yolanda and said: "But, don't you think we should?"

The nurse call system buzzed, cutting short Debbie's pondering. It always came in a dull, monotonous tone. Ted was nearest and leapt to his feet, thankful for this enforced interlude. He checked the display panel.

"It's Jack – Jack Whiteacre. I'll be back in a while."

Mr. Whiteacre was short of breath and starting to feel a little bit apprehensive. The darkness was giving him a feeling of isolation, as it now approached midnight.

"Hello, Jack." Ted knelt down and drew near to Jack gently, to avoid further stress by introducing his presence too abruptly. He could make out the slightly illuminated dome of Jack's balding forehead. As Ted's eyes adjusted to the dim lighting, he made out the man's nose, then traced his other facial features from it: lined, perspiring skin around frightened, bulging eyes. The prominent nose rose and fell slightly with every rapid breath; lips formed an "O" shape, desperately attempting to draw extra oxygen from their surroundings.

"Have you got any chest pain?"

"No, no," Jack replied, "I just feel as if I'm slowly suffocating. Can't sleep."

"If you haven't any pain, should we try a nebulizer for now, Mr. W? I've got your G.T.N. spray in my pocket, in case you do get any chest pain."

"Aye, lad, that's what I need. I keep thinking of bad seams on the pit face again."

Jack's observations were all within acceptable ranges. After about three minutes, as the gushing white swirls of salbutamol vapour started to subside inside the face mask, Jack began to calm down and relax. He soon dozed off, so Ted gently removed the mask and placed it back on the wall mount for the piped oxygen system. He would check that Jack was still settled in half an hour.

Ted knew how dangerous the spiralling effects could be when someone has airways disease combined with heart disease. Breathlessness led to anxiety, and anxiety increased breathlessness. The lack of oxygen to the heart could cause either the heart or pulmonary system to fail, or both.

He noted that it was high time that he checked all was well at the outstations, having not yet heard anything from either. The unspoken rule was, as always: no news is good news.

On 12A, the young but capable Anna was fine.

"Hello, sir." She had heard Ted's footsteps approaching. "We have a nice, quiet crop of customers tonight. They have been so good that I want to keep them all!" Anna waxed lyrical.

She was a drama and dance student at the nearby Athertown University. Ted had tried to persuade her to try a nursing career, seeing her great potential, but she had politely deflected the idea; fame and fortune were the only roads to follow in her well mapped-out scheme of life. Then, when Ted and Lucy had seen her taking a main supporting role in a play sponsored by the University and Arts Council, they had realized her great promise in her chosen field. She was a people person, and loved the old characters on the wards.

As Ted stood in anticipation, she continued; "Miss Wall has been shouting, now and then: *'What are you doing in my wardrobe!? ... Stop digging my garden! ... I know you are trying to find my hidden teapot, with all my money in it!'"*

Ethel Wall was an old-school state-registered nurse herself. They do say that nurses make the worst patients, and Ethel strongly reinforced that theory. When lucid, she called everyone by their surnames.

One evening, she'd had a visit from another pre-World War Two nursing colleague. "Hello, Hodgson," she had exclaimed, "I haven't seen you for ten years!"

"It's only been six months, Wall, but I'll let you off this time. Don't let it happen again."

Ethel spoke in perfect Queen's English. It was a revealing and rewarding snippet of the past, enacted by a rapidly dying breed of completely dedicated spinster vocational nurses. Ethel had been assessed by social services for a placement in a nursing home of her choice. She was a tiny dot of a lady, who peered through or over penny spectacles, usually perched halfway down her petite nose. In the hospital now, staff would repeatedly ask her:

"Would you like a nice, refreshing bath or shower this morning, Miss Wall?"

"Oh, no, thank you, not today; I don't think I will have time to fit that in."

After several days of skilful deferment, staff would put in more effort, trying to persuade her to bathe.

"Now, look," she would say, calmly but firmly, "how would you like it if someone kept coming into your home, trying to get you to do something you don't want to do?"

The valiant, diminutive figure held back all aquarian assailants, through determined conviction, but also, unintentionally, armed with incredible cuteness; this little battler melted hearts.

Ethel had contracted pneumonia in the late spring and had been on 12A for a few months now. She had lived for four years with her sister, who had paid for almost everything: the bills, groceries, taxis; all the things that delicate little sister could simply 'not afford to pay for'." Ethel's fairly tidy pensions were busily distributed into little squirrel-like hoards throughout the large house and, revealed by self-confession now, in the back garden, as well.

Her sister had died last winter, leaving Ethel alone for six months. She almost starved and froze to death as, of course, such a defenceless little thing *"couldn't possibly afford to buy groceries or pay bills; oh, come along now!"* Yet, when a social worker team checked the house on behalf of both absent sisters, they recovered several little bundles of cash totalling over £22,000! A few of the older notes, which Ethel must have brought with her, from one hiding place to another, were no longer even legal tender. Sixty-two full books of Green Shield stamps were also recovered, as were 482 French francs! Sister paid whilst Ethel hoarded. Rainy days obviously had to be paid for as well, at some distant point in Ethel's future!

"Ethel isn't usually as confused as that, is she? Try to get a urine sample from her," Ted instructed; "do a urinalysis stick test, please. If any elements are positive, let me know."

"Will do, boss," Anna chirped. "Are you okay tonight, Ted? You seem a little tense and serious."

"Yes, I've just got a lot on my mind at the moment. I don't want to bother you with it; it's boring stuff." Ted cringed in inward shame at his deceit, well intended though it was.

Suddenly aware of the time, Ted decided to move on, much as he liked talking to Anna.

"Which break do you want tonight, Anna? I'll ask Debbie to cover for you."

"I'd like two to three for my main break, then five to five-thirty for my solitude break, if that's okay."

"That's fine," said Ted. "Okay, I'd better crack on now."

"I can't wait to have a gander at the photos of Claire's new house. Nosey Posey, A.K.A. Old Rosey, that's me."

Ted looked back and forced a reassuring smile, but said nothing.

As Ted's bulk filled then disappeared through the communication corridor entranceway, Anna fretted ever so slightly. Something clearly wasn't good either in Ted's personal life or on the critical wing. She would have to wait over three hours before she could fully investigate.

As Ted trudged through the lengthy link corridor which spanned the outer shell of 12A and 14, he couldn't help mumbling to himself, where no one could hear him: "The shit's going to hit the fan."

On reaching 14's outstation, by the route avoiding the inner wards, he saw that Beth was completing records. But where was Claire? Ted put up a light and jovial smokescreen, to hide his feelings more convincingly this time. "How's things one-third of the way through, kid?"

Beth physically jumped with fright as Ted addressed her. "Eeeek! Ted! What a shock! Why did you come through the service corridor? Are you a porter now?"

"So cheeky for one so young... and so new!" Ted countered. "Well? How's it going out here?"

"Jesse has a persistent cough and Bill can't sleep; he's been pacing up and down. Other than that, all is well."

"That's good. We'll ask the senior houseman if he wants to prescribe something to help Jesse. You will just have to indulge Bill and attempt to keep him as quiet as possible."

"Aww, yes. Bill is missing his wife and family so, with no idea of any discharge date, poor bloke," Beth informed Ted, with sharp insight.

Ted prepared a criticism sandwich: "That's good people skill, Beth; well done. Can I just check with you, though, is coral-pink nail varnish now part of the dress code for this N.H.S. trust?" Ted had a way of scolding his staff in a subtle manner, which usually, but not always, avoided embarrassment, conflict and a lowering of morale.

Beth blushed. She looked up at Ted with appealing, brown puppy eyes, as a form of defence. It worked on the still fairly young Ted, who had as yet only uncovered the tip of the iceberg. For him, the great glacier of female guile at that time lay rooted beneath the ocean of life experience. Ted felt guilty as he glanced away from those large, deep pools, pretending to survey some nearby equipment.

It's part of my job to keep her in line, he bolstered himself, still feeling a touch of guilt for chastening the poor girl, nine years his junior. He hastily justified himself: "It's best that I point it out to you... informally, you know. If Hattie catches you wearing nail varnish, she will have an emergency remedial supervision with you, and put it on your record." Ted did mean well toward the new starter, but was also aware that he was using an unpopular bully figure to deflect from this situation.

"Is she that bad?" Beth now looked at him with anguish. She had only started here six weeks earlier.

I'm making a balls-up of this, Ted thought to himself. "Well... she must have her good points..." he pondered.

Beth relaxed and laughed: "Yeah? Well, let me know when

you find them."

Ted chuckled now, as well. "You're pinching my sarcasm. I'll have to book you into the Sarcasm Isolation Room."

Now they had worked together, to move away from the awkwardness of the situation, Ted at last felt ready to pose the pressing question: "By the way, where's Claire?"

"She just popped into the kitchen, to make us both a cuppa," Beth explained.

"Okay." Ted tried to trivialize his interest in Claire's whereabouts: "Which breaks do you two want? I'll get Zoe to take a break from her ordering work and relieve you."

"Three to four for me, please, and I think Claire likes four to five. I'm going to see Anna for half an hour, for a catch-up."

Ted's anguished mind again pictured excrement, this time being swung about in an improvised sling, hitting a nearby fan and causing unhygienic carnage! Normally, he would see genuine humour in a predicament like this.

Claire hadn't noticed anything wrong with the photos (at least, he thought and hoped), and Yolanda didn't want it pointed out to Claire. Beth and Anna, however, were about to look at the photos and experience what he, Yolanda and Debbie had just been through; they couldn't stop this from happening. What a destructive mess! The clear, so recent memory of that evil face removed any element of humour from the farcical potential of the situation.

On the internal route back to 12A, Ted heard clattering and slamming in the little kitchen. He went to investigate what he thought might be a confused rogue patient. He peered around the corner, into the small room, to see Claire preparing drinks and heating up her supper in the microwave.

"Hi, Claire, are you okay?" he enquired. "I thought a patient – or worse, a senior manager – was on the rampage!"

No laughter was returned, not even a slight smile. "Not really," Claire snapped. Both her sullenness and evident hurt made her voice shaky.

"What's happened?" Ted's mind raced, but he tried to appear calm and naïve.

"I shouldn't be annoyed; it was only an accident. I popped into your main station to collect my photos; Beth, Anna and Zoe haven't seen them yet. Now they never will!"

"Really? Why not?" Ted now sounded astonishingly relieved, despite a poor effort to sound comforting in his tone.

Claire was open and frank with almost everyone, very straightforward in what she said, and she trusted Ted, judging from previous experience. "Yolanda was mashing cardboard waste in the sluice shredder. She reached up to get extra detergent and all of my photos dropped out of her pocket and into the shredder! The careless cow!"

"Oh, no! I'm sure she is as upset as you about it," Ted condoned.

"That would be hard; they were the first photos we've taken of our new house. We only moved in nine days ago! I haven't even bloody well looked at them properly myself, yet – just scanned through them," she sobbed. The tears were welling in her eyes, making light mascara stream down each cheek, like little spears of wet charcoal, compromising her personal dignity. Ted felt a lump in his throat. He placed a comforting hand gently on her shoulder, carefully avoiding invading her personal space. After a few seconds, she turned away to the sink and dabbed her face with cold water, observing the mess of her make-up.

"Can't you get another set from the negatives?" Ted suggested, softly.

"No," Claire responded, bitterly, "I'm fated with these photographs. Dan, my partner, took them to be developed and the negatives were damaged in the process, for some reason – probably because he's a divvy! Then, he had the developed photos in his car for days; I had to lose my temper before he could even be bothered to go to his car and get them for me. Just because some things aren't as important to him as they are to me…"

As Ted listened attentively to Claire's sad but telling

description of events; he now saw the light very quickly: everyone was trying to protect Claire from those horrendous images, and the unimaginable trauma they could cause her.

She looked at Ted, seeing his concern, but also his questioning expression. "I am ranting on a bit, I suppose. Do you think I'm overreacting? I'm very fond of Yolly, really."

Ted rapidly gave small shakes of his head, avoiding eye contact with Claire for the moment, as they stood about five feet apart. "Oh, no, no, not at all... except for calling Yolanda a 'stupid cow', that is. I can understand your disappointment and anger, though; she should have taken more care and kept them out of the working areas."

"That's true; forty-eight photos are far too big to fit safely into one of these uniform pockets! She's mental!"

"But you all love her..."

"Yeah, we do," she admitted; "she's the key figure on these two wards and a great nurse. But, imagine how she would have reacted, if one of us had done that with her holiday photos of Orlando, last month!"

Ted's broad, angular face elevated and took a slight turn, back toward her. His bright, steely, grey-blue eyes resumed contact with the still watery royal-blue eyes of his disgruntled colleague. As Claire calmed, he was able to feel less guilt and more relief. Ted resisted pinching the point of his thin, brown-grey flecked beard, a habit which tended to expose his own anxious moments.

"Are you quiet tonight, Ted, or am I just being extra noisy?"

"A bit of both." Ted now felt bold enough, in his secret relief, to be playful with her.

"Cheeky sod!" She cheered up a little now, and turned to a constructive plan: "I'll just have to get some more taken – exactly the same shots as the destroyed pictures."

Ted worried afresh, that this whole ghastly process might repeat itself!

"Yes, that's it," Claire's enlightened face transformed: "I'm getting a big delivery of new household equipment on Wednesday; I can take new and better photos, when the house looks shipshape and lived in. I'll have a new fan-assisted oven and hob system; new lighting; a new T.V.; new blinds and curtains…"

Ted drew his head back; his chin protruded in unavoidable deep thought. He carefully avoided stroking his beard, so as to appear calm. "I thought your T.V. looked quite new. And it's a good brand."

"It is a fairly good T.V., but I got it free and second-hand; it was just a stop-gap until I could get a new one."

"That seems quite extravagant," said Ted.

"Do you want it?" Claire offered.

"Oh, no, thanks!" he answered, a little too quickly. "I've got a nice one... whenever I get the chance to watch something I like!"

"Oh, I thought you were angling for it," she laughed. "Never mind," she continued, "there is just something about it that I don't like. My friend very kindly gave it to us. She was keeping it as a bedroom spare, which she got when an old man in her street died suddenly, and left some of his estate to her."

Ted felt a sudden ache behind his eyes, radiating toward his temples; a throbbing pulse of pure tension. Claire now sensed Ted's stress level, and gave him a concerned look, though without any trace of suspicion.

Claire was only twenty-four, and had a youthful outlook on life. She was preoccupied, as a Mum of only twenty-two months. She still wore rose-coloured spectacles when viewing many aspects of life and the people around her.

But now Ted was on a fact-finding mission. He wouldn't normally pry, but he did so now, for the best of reasons. "Did you know the old man?" he asked.

"Did I know him? No, he was a strange old recluse," Claire responded.

"Did your friend talk about him, at all?"

"She just said that he kept mainly himself to himself. She used to see him to talk to in his front garden, or now and then in the park, or at a local pub or café. Cathy heard a rumour that he had been in some bother with the police a long time ago, so now he mainly stayed indoors. He was very shy. Why the interest in him?" she queried.

"I'm not sure," said Ted, instantly realizing how lame that sounded.

Claire's head turned to one side, pointedly. Her straightforward, clear-thinking mind was puzzled by his random interest in a stranger. Her head remained in that position, though now for practical purposes: long, slender fingers, very feminine but with bitten nails, stretched open a mint green bobble, ready to receive the long, chestnut hair held tightly in her other hand.

"Erm... somehow I'm just convinced that I've encountered someone like him before. Did Cathy describe what he looked like?"

"Oh, can't I just get to the bathroom and put my face back together?" Claire grumbled.

But Ted wanted a description of him, and he loitered. Fortunately, Claire read this from his body language. "Come with me, if you like. I'm only doing my lippy and eyes."

Ted stood in the bathroom's threshold, while Claire spoke to him through the mirror, as she got her appearance back in order.

"I've seen a couple of photos of him. He was short, for a bloke; only slightly taller than Catherine, and she's about five-foot-four. He was thickset," she recalled.

"What about his face?" Ted pressed for the vital information.

"He wore large-framed, rectangular spectacles. Sometimes he had long, white hair. And, in a couple of photos, he wore a hat—"

"A hat?" blurted Ted, in a reflex reaction.

An overly patient Claire had now had enough of the grilling; "Yes, people do sometimes wear hats!"

"That's interesting," said Ted, "the guy I knew from around there wore an old black trilby, in cold or wet weather."

"A... trilby? I don't know." Claire clearly hadn't heard of this old-fashioned type of hat. "It looked like what the detectives and gangsters wear in old black and white films, but not as smart as theirs. He also wore a long overcoat."

"Maybe I should get one of those detective hats?" Ted laughed, realizing it was now probably time to lighten up.

"Eh? Ahhh... ha-ha... Yeah, I reckon you do," she humoured him.

Ted picked up on Claire's distraction; "Well, Claire, I—"

"Not being rude, Ted, but I want to go now. I need to get back on the floor and these drinks will be getting cold."

"Oh, of course, I'm sorry. Well, I'm pleased you have cheered up a little now, Claire. I had hoped that talking about it would help," he said, in semi-truth about his motives for all the questions.

"Yes, it has, thanks," she smiled politely, then disappeared rapidly around the corner.

Ted reckoned that Claire would go back onto the floor and throw herself into her work, as always. Next time they were on duty together, he was almost certain that she would have a few questions for him, in return! She would probably have taken more photos by then.

He hastened back to the main nurse station, where his benevolent confederates were awaiting his return.

"Are we almost ready to do the next round?" he proposed to Yolanda and Debbie.

He gave them a five-minute debriefing first, of the patients, their young colleagues and, of course, his encounter with Claire. Yolanda listened, saying very little as Ted updated them both. Yolanda, in the role of Yolly, still felt very worried, and also very guilty. Her mind was racing, but she decided to keep her questions and concerns to herself, and concentrate on the ward round.

The three carried out a pretty routine ward round. They made a few people comfortable, and checked one or two essential observations. Still, quiet as this midnight round was attempted, Mr. Sewell was disturbed by their activities.

"I've been dreaming about a fish!" he exclaimed. "This poor fish was sweating and sweating, and swimming and swimming, and sweating again..." It was in fact he who was lathered in sweat, but his temperature was only slightly raised, suggesting that he had no infection. Debbie gave him some oxygen for an hour, and reassured him tenderly; the oxygen should reduce his confusion and agitation. The human brain is very greedy for a large share of the body's total supply of oxygenated blood and, without that supply, anything can happen.

Tiring now, it being 00:52, the three beckoned to the god Caffeine for a well-needed boost, before setting about their extensive paperwork. They briefly reflected on the patients – a routine task – then, almost inevitably, tonight's star topic quickly surfaced again.

Yolanda, forever the pragmatist, but with a little mystique interwoven, had decided on a coping strategy for all three of them. The others sometimes teased her as being a frustrated doctor or social worker, always wanting to prescribe life remedies to those around her. Yolanda accepted this in-house jibing from those she respected, and who had earnt the right to be familiar, but woe betide any newcomer or "outsider" who tried to jump on the bandwagon; they would be in deep shit indeed, and probably burn any future bridges with her.

"I think we need to discuss our views and ideas about Claire's pictures now, then draw a line under it all."

Yolanda was a latent socialist, through and through, but in discussions on non-medical matters affecting the staff, she could be as tyrannical as a Queen Bess! Ted and Debbie both nodded along, and all three of them looked at each other concurringly.

Surprisingly, it was Debbie who made the next big contribution to this "final" discussion. Debbie was very down to earth, essentially quiet, but thoughtful, and this was reflected in her diplomatic views. "We can't in any way explain those two horrible images. We all saw and felt the same terror. By a lucky fluke—" she glanced at Yolanda "—only us three and Claire's Darren seem to know about them.

"We can't discuss this in front of anyone else in here; this station is the safest place to talk without the chance of someone eavesdropping." She stopped to reflect now, looking down at the split in the side of her left shoe, but she was allowed no time to recap, as the artillery queen was about to speak:

"That's right, Claire must never know," insisted Yolanda; "my Cancerian star sign needs us all to be drawn in protection around her."

Ted now ventured to speak, before the others chipped in again: "I'm only playing Devil's advocate here, but does Claire not have the right to—"

"No!" Yolanda swiftly rebuked. "Not over something as damaging as this, Ted."

"Well, hang on…" Ted saw a need to assert his stake in the debate. He knew he could do this partly by pulling rank; Yolanda was a junior nurse, capped at what was then termed a "D grade", having recently converted from the old state-enrolled nurses. "I agree with you, Yolanda, but this is too important not to discuss the options. It will probably help with closure for us, too," he reasoned.

"Mmm… well, I don't really see the need for it, but come on, then." Yolanda knew that she had to indulge this challenge, through respect for Ted's status as an E grade. He was, however, threatening her protective crab environment; Ted had better not try to stop her from extending her protective claw movements, to gather up those most in need of her armoured carapace! Another problem for a Zodiac believer like herself was that this man was a Piscean: very influential in her domain; a lithe fish darting around in her maritime environment.

Debbie instinctively positioned herself in the role of referee; "Finish what you were going to say, Ted."

Ted looked at Yolanda. Her fine lips, adorned with a subtle purple tone, were pursed and stylish, but also defiant. Her gold-rimmed spectacles were quite low on her nose. Above them, her now stern eyes were mobilized for battle. Her brood was not to be threatened by any fish's foray! Ted the human took up the opportunity to test her tough defences:

"I just want to be one hundred per cent sure that it wouldn't be better for us to tell Claire about it. What if, in a couple of weeks' time, we are sitting looking at shocking images again? Or, worse still, Claire sees the evil man herself this time?"

"I see your point," Yolanda quickly conceded, "but there were only two awful images, and the T.V. was in seven of the photos, so we can only hope that it was a one-off. Besides, Ted, you told us that she intends to get rid of that T.V., which seems to be the main source of the evil. Hopefully it was just an optical illusion, caused by a play of light on a television programme?" Yolanda knew full well now that she was betraying her own principles, diluting the memory for the greater scheme of things; she didn't really believe for one second that what they had seen was an optical illusion. She had seen a demonic entity and she knew it.

Ted clung to his purpose; "And the story of the old man who previously owned the T.V.?"

Yolanda resumed her practical, protective mission; "Even if

we think that was him in the T.V., we couldn't do anything about it, except to try and protect Claire Bear. Maybe it is only in the T.V.; it will be gone next week."

After a couple more minutes of ping-pong debate between Ted and Yolanda, with Debbie as a de facto referee, it was time to knuckle down to some paid work.

"Well, I've got to go and update two care plans," sighed Debbie.

After thirty seconds of silence between Ted and Yolanda, with their mediator gone now, Yolanda arose from her computer chair. "I'll go and print off tomorrow's charts and handover sheets in the I.T. room."

"Okay," replied Ted.

She had moved a few rapid steps when, at the threshold of the nurse station, she heard the half-expected questioning voice of her relative newcomer "boss", once more:

"Yolanda... how did you get all of Claire's photos into your uniform pocket?"

Her almost silhouette-like, Moorish figure stopped dead in its tracks in the doorway. Turning slowly around again, into better light, Yolanda looked at Ted. Her eyes and lips now worked in unison, to produce a spontaneous smile fuelled by mischief. "I'm a curvy size twelve," she winked.

Ted looked up with a vanquished expression, without

attempting to gain further confirmation of the deed in question; he knew he would get nowhere. An exasperated but amused sigh from Ted ended the proceedings. There was no way all of those photos could have been shredded in one bundle by accident.

Ted may be the new night-king of 12A and 14, but Yolanda was definitely a higher queen to all of the persons therein.

IV

Ted, Lucy, Native Americans and Aliens

Ted pulled onto the driveway, behind Lucy's car.

His mind had been racing throughout the forty-minute journey home. His thoughts were going around in circles, more than they were helping him to make sense of those images. Swirling at the centre of his thoughts was that horrific detached face.

He tried to concentrate as he turned off the engine. This was another beautiful morning, so perhaps he and Lucy could have a nice breakfast in the garden, before he went to bed.

Focus on this morning, normality and your lovely wife, Ted meditated. *You managed to function at work well enough. When you are alone you overthink everything; you always over-egg the pudding. You did this a lot when you lived alone for those two long years. Outwardly you feel calm enough, so just clear your mind and relax... Relax!*

Ted saw Penny, with her nose pressed against the sitting-room window. She was quickly joined by Florin... Oh, and there was Rosie, as well, her darker outline camouflaged against the black leather chair, in contrast to the white and pale grey of the other little people. Opening the porch door, Ted was met by the onrush of two Cavalier King Charles spaniels and, the greatest challenge, a bouncing young Bedlington terrier. These were the little people. Florin, their Cavalier Blenheim, ran around in large, rapid circles, whooping and whining delightedly like a tiny, red and white Native American pony. Her main nickname was "Crazy Horse", because of this and the fact that, petite though she was, she would simply charge through any obstacle or hurdle to get to food. Rosie, a six-year-old, black and tan cavalier, gave a more time-honoured canine welcome, with the decorum of a "spaniel lady". Though small, she was more solidly built than Florin, and had a calm "type B" approach to life. Then, there was Penny... What to say of Penelope Fry? Always in competition with the much older Rosie, she leapt up, using her long, whippet-like legs, to get most of Ted's attention. Bedlington terriers are very dexterous with their front paws; they use them to wrap around your arm, and cling on for a hug – she always did this, to greet both Ted and Lucy. If she used the arm of a chair as her base, she was able to whisper a strange canine message of affection into Ted's ear, cleaning it at the same time.

Lucy had been up since seven to let the dogs outside, after a night of furry cuddles in her husband's absence. She must have popped back to bed, Ted guessed.

Whilst the pooches were in the back garden, Yorkie the cat, ever the opportunist, slinked in through the front door, as Ted took the rubbish out. Yorkie was always well dressed; whether for breakfast or dinner, he wore his tuxedo outfit as usual: white socks, a white chest on an otherwise black apparel. He was a most distinguished and elegant dining guest.

He looked even smarter in his attire and decorum, when contrasted against the crazy canine mob marauding around in great excitement; forty-eight sharp little claws often clattered back and forth at high speed, in two minutes of mayhem and excitement. If the dogs caught the cat on the floor, he would be flattened like an old game hunter's trophy hide, and have to make his escape at the first opportunity, onto the benches in the kitchen, fighting – mostly with retracted claws – against young Florin and Penny. The more mature Rosie remained ladylike, having long forgotten how she used to do exactly the same thing, until she was at least three years old! Now, she would stay out of the skirmish with dignity.

Yorkie had several different planned and rehearsed routes available, each time he returned to the house. But this time he couldn't believe his luck: not one canine hooligan in sight! Purring in triumph and contentment, he proudly sat in position to enjoy his breakfast of cat meat and biscuits. He felt even more smug when he heard little scratching sounds at the firmly closed back door.

Having seen to the menagerie of pets, Ted couldn't wait to go upstairs and tell Lucy all about the night he had just endured. Reaching the foot of the stairs, he already discerned the graceful outline of Lucy's head and shoulders, against the bright sunlight penetrating the toilet window.

"Hello, Bear," she exclaimed, slightly sleepy, but enthusiastic.

"Even on the throne you still look gorgeous, missus."

"Mmm... flattery might get you somewhere, sometime, mister," replied a still sleepy but teasing Lucy. "What sort of a night have ya had?"

"Nursing-wise, fairly routine; we are under-occupied, but a few people are quite poorly. But, something really awful happened involving one of the staff," Ted recounted.

He knew his wife held grounded views on anything supernatural, paranormal, ghostly, or otherwise generally not of this Earth, but it would still be good therapy to get it off his chest, and file events deeper and hopefully duller within his memory bank.

"Oh, no, are they okay?" Lucy started to awaken fully now, and sat up on the toilet, instead of perched forward, as she had been, seeming about to fall forward and dunch her nose off the floor at any second now.

"Yes, she's fine. But it's something I need to tell you about in detail. Are you getting up now?"

"Yeah, I want to spend some time with you this morning," she cooed, in her smooth, well-spoken tones.

"Okay, Poshie Pants," Ted responded, with a slight undertone of excitement in his voice. "I've let Yorkie Porkie in and fed him. I presume the girls need feeding?"

"They've been fed – and don't let them tell you otherwise," Lucy instructed and teased.

Ted's stock response to this in-house joke was: "I know. They never tell me what they've been up to whilst I've been away." He'd never met a dog who wouldn't let you feed it twice, if you could be foxed into doing so.

He let the three musketeers back indoors. Florin looked straight up at her "Daddy" and belched as she trotted in; further evidence that she had already eaten. Ted stuck the kettle on and popped three slices of bread into the toaster: two for him and one to satiate his wife's modest appetite. She would still leave the crusts, then say ninety minutes later that she was starving.

He smiled as he watched the woolly grey outline of Penny, poised on the arm of the sofa, patiently waiting to pounce on Florin. She would wait, motionless, for a long time, until

Florin was distracted from the Mexican standoff; then the Bedlington's long legs would spring into action, bringing her down on top of the little Cavalier. It was very entertaining to Ted. He could understand now why Bedlington terriers had been bred specially to ambush rats in the coal mines of northern England.

Heavy but eager steps trundled down the stairs.

"Good morning, kipper," Lucy yawned out the words.

"Kipper?" enquired a puzzled Ted. "Do I stink of fish or something?"

"Yes, stinker, get your arse in that shower!" she cackled, for effect.

"Maybe next Tuesday, mate!" came Ted's reply. Both laughed.

"Let's sort our toast out, then you can tell me your story," she suggested. "Ooh, that's a lovely strong cuppa," she commended her hubby, between sips.

A minute or two of munching at the breakfast bar followed, then they retired to the sitting room, armed with cups of tea and coffee to keep them alert. Ted poured out the full tale of Claire, the little boys in the photos and, of course, those horrendous images of the evil man in the T.V.

Lucy's initial response surprised him: "Eurgh! That sounds awful! It's strange how the mum didn't notice those pictures, even briefly flicking through."

"It is," Ted agreed. "Lucky as well, though."

"Well, if you think it all through," logical Lucy piped up, quickly, "it must be some kind of optical illusion. I think the T.V. was on and the strange image was being broadcast on a daytime programme—"

"But—"

"Just a minute, voodoo man," she snapped, slightly irritated, "I've listened to you for over five solid minutes... Right, there must be an explanation for it. Remember Stella's strange holiday photos, last summer?"

"It was an all-time record for you: five whole minutes of silence. I certainly do remember those photos from America," Ted recalled, with conviction. "If you had seen these ones, though, before they were destroyed... all three of us were left emotionally devastated, for quite some time. It's hard to describe, but it must be... erm... like a form of... being haunted."

"I'm waking up and you are tiring," Lucy observed.

"Yeah, I'm knackered. In fact, I would say I'm 'Donald Ducked'," complained Ted. He added a deliberate tone to his voice, as if to put across the message to Lucy that she should realize he had now been awake for almost seventeen hours!

"You'll be asleep in ten minutes," her complaint persisted.

"I don't think so," he contested; "I will take about an hour and a half; this coffee is starting to kick in now. Are you going to knock us up a full English?"

"Nope, sorry, I haven't got eggs, bacon or black pud, and I'm almost skint until next week," Lucy sighed.

"Oh, damn." Disappointed, Ted suddenly felt very hungry. He continued the conversation, all the same: "Why would Yolanda destroy the photos, if they weren't seriously showing some sort of apparition?"

"I'm sure it must have looked awful, Bear Pear, but didn't she claim that they were destroyed by accident?"

"She *claimed* it was an accident, but I know her better than that."

At that, Lucy looked at her husband, but she said nothing. *Knows her better than that, does he? After eight months, and a couple of shifts here and there? Monitoring this one, methinks!* Lucy closed one eye and pouted her lips, her slender, oval head tilted slightly against a knee, drawn up for defensive support against this onslaught in the morning. Her tiny chin almost disappeared into the thin veneer of loose denim. "And... you obviously don't think it was?"

"I know full well it wasn't. She gave me a non-verbal sign that she had put them down the shredder deliberately. I'm sussing Yolanda out now."

This time, following the further remark, Lucy could hold back the question no longer: "Do you fancy her?" Lucy's head now levelled against both drawn-up knees. The diminutive chin was now completely submerged, allowing only full, dark-red lips to converse.

"No, I like and respect her, and she is an attractive *older* lady."

"Yeeessss?"

"No. I've never really thought about it, but no, I don't," a slightly dishonest Ted told his beloved wife.

"Good. I can kinda tell, anyway." She presented a cheeky mock grin, with full lips, revealing perfectly white, slightly prominent teeth – a unique smile that Ted had been drawn to, as so, so lovely Lucy. The smile ended their conflict through chemistry.

Ted did find Yolanda attractive, but only from afar. He was more than happy with his drop-dead gorgeous wife.

"Now then, Teddy, stop thinking about sexy nurses, you fierce, troublesome cuddly bear! Let's finish this debate, then enjoy some relaxation."

"Aye, let's, Mrs. Little Green Monster Munch!"

He tried to focus back on what seemed to be a degeneration into rambling, rather than the compact, hard-hitting story and debate he had wanted to deliver. The Lucy factor had taken the edge off, as had waves of fatigue. He threw out another one of his standard one-liners: "Oh, where are my matchsticks?"

"To prop open your bloodshot blues," she laughed.

"Exactly. Okay, well, I know you are coming from the starting point of a sceptic on anything like this – I used to be exactly the same – but when you start to experience the unexplainable, it makes you more open-minded." He paused for her reply.

Lucy tried to rationalize what was, to her, still irrational, from Ted's viewpoint. She was quite good at empathizing, and knew that he was a very rational person in general. She admired him greatly as a nurse and for his magical relationship with elderly people. She wanted him to soon be the father of her children, no matter how much he stalled over it; he would be a brilliant, wacky dad. And he would be a dad quite soon. *A lot sooner than he wants to be, if I have my way,* she thought. *I will keep working on him in womanly ways,* she dreamed and schemed. Smiling, for reasons unknown to her spouse, she now tried to be more open-minded, without giving up her true convictions. "I believe that something awful has had an effect on you, darls – obviously your workmates, as well. I just think that it must have a rational, and probably boring, explanation."

He tried again, and his woman genuinely wanted to support him. Where would this end? "Remember when I told you about my weird experience, on my night-duty module, as a student nurse?"

"I do, I sure do," Lucy concurred. "That was just before we met, so I think it was part of your box of chat-up tricks at that time. Bears are clever and resourceful, aren't they?"

Lucy's hand now came up, flexing her delicate fingers then cupping her palm, to bring fresh support to her face. Her still drawn-up legs were now starting to go into a cramp. She put them back down to the floor and sat upright in the chair; only her propped-up head remained lazy, but thoughtful.

Ted was gradually declining into the sofa. His body needed to start resting, but his overstimulated brain had a little mileage left. Almost in a mirror image of Lucy, his large hand shovelled his head, as his fingers ran through his dark brown, grey-flecked hair.

Deep-hazel eyes peered lovingly at him. "You could do with a haircut soon," Lucy noted.

"Oh, come on, Mother! Do you just want to talk about the price of cheese?" he said, sardonically. *She likes me with long hair, but she also wants me to get it cut! Women!* He shook his head.

Lucy gave no quarter. "The price of clothes and shoes would be more interesting." Her mind had warmed up now, helped by eight hours of sleep and a very strong cup of tea with two sugars, the teabag still bobbing around in her cup, permeating its caffeine stimulus.

"I won't bore you with that again, then," remarked Ted. "Stella's photos are probably more relevant here, but not in any way as sinister."

"Come on, then, talk it through to further your cause," Lucy challenged him, noticing that his mind was alert again.

"Okay." Ted prepared to recap on Stella's experience with some strange photos. Stella was a workmate and now a good friend of Lucy. They occasionally had dinner or a coffee meet up; her fiancé Andy sometimes came, too. "Indulge me, then," Ted instructed, "just for two minutes.

"Stella showed us the snaps of her trip to the Grand Canyon, in May last year. As we both know and saw, one photograph had a superimposed image of an old man's hand, holding Red Indian runes."

Ted studied his wife for a moment, as he caught his breath and collected his thoughts. He noticed her fingers now gently tapping against the side of her temple. Lucy was either thinking, getting slightly anxious or both.

"He was a Native American, but do go on." The tapping continued. The remark suggested cynical thought, rather than anxiety.

"Right, I will," a determined Ted continued. "Another

picture showed a superimposed dreamcatcher, again in the old man's hand. Then, there was the picture of a sweeping prairie, complete with cacti and tumbleweed; a classic Wild West stage. This time you saw the old man's face outlined: long hair, calm, meditating face, resigned to the powers of life and nature. He knew about that land. He knew that it could never belong to man. All men of all times could only pass through this land, in turn becoming ghosts, as it remained forever. A wise old man from a culture all but swept away."

Lucy stopped tapping and extended the same hand outward, open, in a "game over" gesture. Ted almost seemed to be narrating the words of another. Though interesting, she also found this a little disturbing. To take the focus off of the spiritual, she dropped her bombshell: "Stella told me later that it was just a hoax." Lucy's other arm extended in an open, supporting stance, to complete the kill.

"What?" Ted was surprised. "Stella doesn't seem the type of person to play childish pranks like that."

Lucy drew back in the chair again, sinking slightly into the black leather. Her skin looked extra pale, milky against her dark surroundings. She crossed her slender legs, pointing the crossed leg toward Ted; her open, slippered foot was now only a few inches from his face.

He looked dumbfounded for a second, then regained his

poise. He was well used to these contests with Lucy. "Those slippers are a bit pongy. You don't normally have stinky feet," he said.

"The young'uns keep pinching them off my feet, or out of the porch, and using them as a toy, until I tell them off and get them back. They are getting pooch slobber all over them." Lucy put on a mock expression of solemnity, but with a slightly scrunched-up nose, which betrayed the desired expression.

It was a bright morning now. The rare north England hot summer sun was about to bless this bleak part of the planet for a ninth consecutive day! Lucy's hazel eyes responded to our star's generosity with a blaze of pure dark green.

"Well? How did she get them done?" Ted's debate had started to flounder in a new wave of fatigue. This combined with an admiration for his wife's amazing eyes and fine features.

"She didn't. I'm pulling your plonker, you plonker!"

Ted was taken aback, but was also amused more than indignant. "You little shit!" he said.

Lucy grinned and chuckled. "Take a good look at your dumb mug," she said, in merciless triumph.

Ted mustered new energy, borne of revenge. He grabbed her foot, pulled off her slipper, and proceeded to spank the sole of her bare foot with it. "Bad girls must be chastised! You know the rules! Baaad gaaaal!" he laughed.

Lucy squealed and laughed until the two merged into one fun, feminine sound! It combined with her action, as she kicked at Ted's skilfully manoeuvring, slipper-clad hand. As he tired and lost proficiency, she kicked the slipper spiralling into mid-air. As it landed near the fireplace, Penny pounced from the arm of the sofa; the unfortunate slipper, still on the shelf of a shop a week earlier, was now transformed into a rat or a rabbit, as the lean whippet terrier shook it rapidly from side to side, then hurled the prey through the air again, to break its neck.

"I give up on that slipper," Lucy giggled now, resigned in frustration.

Though the slipper was now out of the scene, Lucy held firmly onto Ted's wrist. This prevented him from tickling the sole of her foot, as a secondary playful punishment.

"You are not out of the woods yet, Miss Lucy Jane Teacake!" Ted's voice now quivered with laughter.

"Don't you dare call me Jane Teacake! You're the big fairy around here!"

Both spouses were now distracted, well and truly, reverting back to their playful courtship days. This relaxed them both and they needed that – especially Ted, on this particular morning.

"Penelope!" Lucy bellowed. "If Dad is telling me off, I'm going to tell you off!" She took off her second slipper, now realizing its worthlessness. She brandished it at the terrier, as if a second rodent, coming to save the life of its kin. Penny took up the challenge and proficiently leapt onto the second "rabbit".

"I'm feeling *very* playful now, Mr. Fry!" Lucy's eyes and body language meant business.

"Well... my batteries have suddenly gone back up to about twenty per cent, Mrs. Fry. Shall we play?"

Lucy leapt from the chair, taunting and tantalizing her still lounging husband. "Last one up the stairs is a limp old fart!" she challenged.

Ted jumped up and ran after the giggling nymph, as her willowy form sprinted up the staircase; that was one of his more endearing names for her: "Willow". Three little dogs ran after them. On occasions like this, much to their surprise, the rather pampered pets would be left waiting on the landing, outside the door of the marital bedroom.

A loving and satisfying romantic romping session followed. Afterward, Lucy and Ted fell fast asleep.

When Ted awoke, he looked at the clock: wow! Nearly six hours' sleep! *Sex is a brilliant tranquillizer,* he noted, *I don't normally sleep that soundly.*

He stretched out in bed for a minute; a feeling of pure physical and mental glory! Feeling relaxed and refreshed, he sprang out of bed to go take a piss. He was motivated further by the inviting aroma of fresh ground coffee from the kitchen.

"Afternoon, darls," a lively, richly feminine voice called from below, as welcoming as the coffee.

Ted replied: "Oh, hellooo there! Hey, can I order you again for the same time tomorrow? Miss... Smith, isn't it?"

"No, hopeless memory, it's Miss Samantha Watson. You can, but I'm very expensive, mind."

Ted took a quick shower and trimmed his thin beard. He was finished in about fifteen minutes. It wasn't quick enough.

"What are you doing up there, Bear? Your coffee is down here for ya, going cold."

"I'm just trimming my beard and getting dressed," replied Ted.

A few seconds later, hurried, heavy, familiar steps came bounding up the stairs, accompanied once more by the twelve paws of the little disciples.

"Now who's fairy Jane Teacake?" Lucy taunted. "I wish you would get rid of that stupid excuse for a beard. You know

I don't like them."

"So, I have to have longish hair to keep you and my mother happy, but I can't have a beard? Long hair but no beard makes me look a bit feminine," complained Ted.

"Don't be daft. It looks sexy on ya! It could be well worth your while to get rid of it!" Lucy bargained.

"And, who would make it worth my while?" he enquired.

"That Miss Samantha Watson, for one! Possibly me, too."

Ted was convinced; "I'll shave it off next time I'm off work. Deal?"

"Deal," she said, excitedly, with a tiny jolt of energy.

"After your coffee, can we go into town for an early dinner?" Lucy asked, hopefully.

"Erm... will we have time for that?" Ted wondered.

Lucy had the plan ready: "I will walk the dogs after you go to work. That should give us nearly three hours."

"Deal number two," Ted smiled.

"Yay!" Lucy was growing excited now.

She was a very youthful twenty-six. Living independently since virtually her sixteenth birthday, she had a maturity in practical living. She also had a childlike level of excitement and energy, which was often dampened by life events or hormone cycles. She could at times be a little too hyper, when Ted wanted peace and quiet, or wanted to read or watch the

T.V. In the broad picture of life, however, Ted loved this enthusiastic and outgoing side to Lucy. Lucy was also an avid reader of some of the lighter classics, as well as more serious novels; she was often reading three books before she finished the first one, but only a really bad choice of novel would be discarded partly read. Both of them were very hedonistic and also loved to travel.

Lucy drove into town as part of the deal. About two minutes into the journey, Ted returned to the earlier, unfinished debate about Stella's photos, which had been interrupted so agreeably that morning!

"I still think the photos of the Native American man and the sinister old man are both part of something beyond human comprehension," he suddenly declared. "I'm convinced that —"

"Ducks!" Lucy exclaimed.

"What? Oh, yes, aren't they cute?" Ted smiled. A mother duck waddled proudly and protectively near the roadside, followed by a perfect line of four tiny, brown ducklings. She was taking them from the village pond, across to the gentle riverbank, for further training.

"Anyhoo…" Ted persisted, "what about these photos?"

"One set of exposures got mixed up with another during development, or in the camera," Lucy replied.

"You know that could only be possible if Stella isn't telling the truth. She and Andy both said, quite emphatically, that they did not see any Native American characters, let alone take any pictures of them."

"I just can't accept it, darls." Lucy glanced at her husband, as she slowed at a junction. "There isn't enough evidence to make it something supernatural, or whatever."

"This is just like your close-mindedness about the possibility of aliens existing," mused Ted.

"Aliens? Have we ever discussed that in any depth?"

"We have. I think we were both under the influence at the time," he reminded her.

"Ah, well, there ya go. Briefly – and I mean *briefly* – refresh my memory, please," Lucy instructed, "before we park up."

Ted took in a deep breath, ready to start his rapid mini-lecture. "My belief is that there must be aliens out there in the universe – lots of them. The human mind can't even comprehend infinity, and space is believed to be endless; the sheer number of stars and planets suggests that there must be more systems out there, where life has occurred and evolved." He looked at Lucy without hope of agreement; he remembered the previous run of this debate.

"What you looking at?" she said, concentrating on the road ahead.

"I'm finished. What is your opinion?" enquired Ted.

"Well," she deliberated, without enthusiasm, "if I haven't seen real evidence of aliens, then I don't believe that they exist."

Ted's response was reflexive, because he had thought about it a lot: "We have never encountered alien lifeforms because space is too immense to be able to travel far enough, or in the right direction, for us ever to meet up."

Lucy scowled slightly. "All of your space heroes on T.V. and films manage it."

Ted objected: "That's just science fiction."

"So is your mumbo jumbo. We're pulling in now." Her voice indicated that she wished to draw an end to the subject.

But, Ted got in his final parting shot: "Imagine putting a man in a rowing boat in London, and sending him to row to New York City. Then imagine putting a man in a rowing boat in New York City, with his destination London, across the three-thousand-mile expanse of the Atlantic Ocean. Apart from the fact that they almost certainly don't have the technology to succeed, more importantly to my theory, what would be the likelihood of them ever passing each other on that journey? That's why we will never meet aliens with our foreseeable technology."

Ted thought about adding that mankind would probably destroy itself and all other lifeforms on Earth before we ever got around to distant space travel, but decided to leave out this negative footnote to his theory.

"It just reminds me of *The Bible*," said Lucy; "just because you believe it, doesn't mean that it really happened."

"True. Very true. But some things in *The Bible* have been given a logical explanation. I have mathematics on my side; the law of probability," Ted summarized.

"You've got a bee in ya bonnet on your side; buzz, buzz! Now, give it some time off and get ya other friend ready for action."

"I thought I'd already done that," Ted replied, smuttily.

Lucy tutted; "I meant your wallet, naughty man!"

After a good dinner, to complete a great day, Ted again resigned himself to the inevitable, and set off on the familiar journey to work. *The endless cycle of work and play goes on,* he sighed.

On the journey, he reflected on a number of things, especially Lucy. Lucy was younger than him, and had a more affluent upbringing, but probably a less happy one. Her father had been away, working for oil and third-world technology companies as an accountant, for many of her childhood years. She would have loved to have been a Daddy's girl, but was deprived of that, from about the age of eight to leaving home. She clashed with her mum much of the time, an eccentric and flighty natured woman, who didn't provide a very stable home life for Lucy or her sister, Fey. Lucy always felt that her mum favoured and had more time for the two brothers, who were much older than the girls.

Lucy was very cheerful, outgoing and hardworking, but her early years had already brought her, in her mid-twenties, to be a realist over many issues. She had once told Ted a simple but very effective story, which showed her sound grip on reality, most of the time. She used to take the two family dogs for a countryside walk, from about the age of ten, and so often she would just get back through the front door when the heavens would open; she would stroke her dry pets and laugh at her luck. When this happened about ten times over a couple of months, Lucy started to believe that she was impervious to rain when she had the pets with her. She told this to Fey and persuaded her, one leaden-sky afternoon, to come along, even though Fey thought they were about to be soaked. Sure enough, not more than half a mile into the planned two-mile walk, the heavens opened in a cruel, torrential early-autumn downpour. The walk was abandoned, and the two soaking wet girls had to wring out their clothes, whilst wet pets soaked them again, as they shook themselves dry. Lucy's myth was shattered! It was but one of many disappointments for her in her early years.

Beneath these deep thoughts, Ted felt surprisingly carefree and cheerful, considering that he was only about to commence the second of four hard nights of work. He credited Lucy with helping him to achieve this positive frame of mind.

Then he reached the three-tunnel system in the road once more. After the customary look at nearby stationary vehicles, he found that he wasn't making up his usual dodgy song lyrics. Was he cured?

Instead, though, he soon started to become preoccupied once more with the two images he had seen in the photos last night. *Oh, shit!*

He put his head down, obscuring his face with cupped hands. *Perhaps my stupid singing isn't such a bad thing after all,* he told himself.

V

In Yolanda's Worlds

Eleven days had now passed since the "Night of the Evil Floating Head". Yet now, as Ted once more pulled into the car park at the hospital, he was slightly apprehensive. He was mindful that this was the first time almost all the same staff would be on duty as had been that night, including Yolanda and Debbie.

As he got out of the car, the near-twilight summer sun still provided cheering warmth. A few territorially spaced birds delivered their calming evensong, in combination with the weather, to ease Ted's tension even further. The real world was much stronger than the spiritual, he assured himself.

A slight feeling of déjà vu overcame Ted, as the first person he saw was again Yolanda. The feeling was negated slightly by the fact that, this time, he had entered a reception area which was quiet and deserted. He had also changed into his uniform this time, before speaking to her. Yolanda had a look of sorrow on her face, as she came close to Ted, walking slowly but deliberately toward him. He feared, as he observed her approach, that there had been unknown repercussions regarding the evil man in the T.V., though he had heard little bad news on previous nights this week.

"Ted, I don't want to broadcast this down the ward, but Mr. Whiteacre passed away suddenly, in the early hours of this morning."

"Oh, no, that's a real shame," Ted sighed.

"I knew you were fond of him, Ted, you old softy," Yolanda comforted him.

"I was. Another old miner fades away; it's like another historical character has gone forever."

"It is," Yolanda agreed. "Our World War One lads are nearly all gone now, as well. It said in the paper the other day that there are less than a thousand men alive in the world who fought in that war."

"Hello, gang," Jim interjected, "do you fancy coming through to the office for a medical lesson, once your history lesson is finished?"

"Sarcastic bugger!" Yolanda muttered, when Jim was just about out of earshot.

The handover of twenty-one patients took about fifteen minutes; the average was only about eight to ten. The ward had filled up quite a lot. Four patients were very ill, all recent admissions; one man had come in with hypothermia, after being found by the police in a bus shelter, at four in the morning. He had been caught in the rain, then fallen asleep, with the same effect as if he had frozen in winter. He hadn't realized or cared that, even in the summer, this was dangerous – especially for a man of seventy-two. Ward 12A had a special hypothermia treatment side room, in which the temperature could be manually controlled by the care team. He was now recovering well, after almost twenty-four hours on the ward.

Jim gave an interesting and detailed report. He was a very experienced charge nurse, with an informal, modern approach to management, leading mainly by his personality, backed by great knowledge and experience. He was a joker, who could sometimes be a little too sarcastic toward others, but stood with his staff, first and foremost. He also had an unsurpassed acumen for the role he knew so well. Recent managerial changes, and a redefining of the role of ward charge nurses and sisters, set out to make them managers before nurses, and at times, lately, it was making Jim tired and disillusioned. He now had to worry about budgets, audits, accountability, time and motion surveys, and even whether or not his patients should be called "customers", "consumers" or "service users"! Head-exploding problems indeed! Jim saw most of this as bullshit, as did most of his nurses and auxiliary nurses. He was spending as much time in meetings, lately, as he was on his own ward, and recently the pressure had been getting to him.

He was having to annoy members of staff, some of whom he had known in the hospital for up to twelve years, by telling them not to waste materials, because of his budget restraints. These days, he was openly talking about going into the school of nursing to teach – he would be first-class at that.

At the end of the report, he broke further gloomy news to Ted and the other staff. His eagle-like face protruded well forward of a long, very lean body, as his white, knee-length doctor's coat snagged against the chair leg, threatening to tear under the strain, as in a quiet but angry tone, he stated: "I've been asked to manage both 12A and 14, when Sister Dene leaves in three months' time." His pale-blue eyes darted around, beady from alarm and self-imposed guilt. "I have a feeling I will be lumbered with her elderly outpatients' extended duties, as well." None of Jim's characteristic wisecracks ended the statement – a sure sign that he was pissed off.

"Will we get any extra help and support when you are elsewhere?" asked Anna. She could immediately tell by Jim's despondent expression that the answer was either negative or, at best, unknown. Jim read her face and those of his other key night staff, in return. He didn't need to give a verbal reply.

Ted was as sad as the other staff, understanding that they would be seeing less and less input and support from Jim soon.

As he looked at the staff, Ted suddenly noticed that Yolanda's left hand, scratching her nose, was bandaged from palm to just below the elbow.

Heavy-hearted after the bad news, the teams prepared for their regular duties, as they did at the beginning of every shift.

"What happened to your hand, Yolanda?" asked Ted.

"I was in the sluice, the night after we last worked together, and the rinsing water suddenly came out abnormally hot, scalding my hand and wrist. I went over to A-and-E for a special dressing."

"Bloody hell!"

"Yeah, I had to take three nights off. Didn't you know?" she asked.

"I knew you were off sick, but there were so many different theories floating about as to why?"

"No surprises there." Yolanda raised her eyebrows.

Debbie piped in, now: "Yes, I told everyone that me, her and a few other friends were on a girls' night out, and we asked Yolly to pay for a round of drinks, and she fainted."

Yolanda rapped Debbie across the back of the head. "That cheek will cost you one nice hairstyle, lady!"

"It already has, by the looks of it," Debs moaned, looking in the nearby mirror to correct her locks.

"Make yourself useful, dear Debbie Dips," Yolanda half

requested and half ordered: "check that Anna knows Mr. Gillingham has to be at Medical Physics for his tests at nine a.m. tomorrow. We have to fast him from midnight; clear water only up to six a.m., then nothing."

"Okay," Debbie agreed, hoping for a catch-up with Anna anyway.

"Are you okay to do the rounds with that arm?" Ted fretted.

"Yes, I'll just have to be careful that no one grabs onto it; that would hurt!"

"Okay," Ted said, only semi-convinced. "I think we need to keep you away from the sluice, as well; it seems to be cursing you lately."

Yolanda gave Ted a knowing look, and saw one returned in his eyes. She knew for sure now that he knew.

"Claire has had two sick days, as well," she ventured.

"I know," said Ted, "I took her call to say that she had also injured her hand."

"Do you know how it happened?" Yolanda's question was loaded with knowledge – as the oracle should be.

"Actually, no, I didn't press her on that; you aren't supposed to ask when someone rings in sick."

"Do you want to know?" Again, her tone was suggestive.

"Of course. Please enlighten me," Ted replied, frankly.

Yolanda's dramatic expression reanimated her face, which

had thus far in the shift held a slightly troubled expression. "Well, Claire and her partner were loading a car trailer, to take some unwanted furniture and old electricals up to the council rubbish tip."

"Oh, yes," Ted noted, "she said she was going to update everything."

"That's right," Yolanda continued; "she told you she wanted rid of that dreaded T.V. Well, she was helping her partner lift the T.V. and she lost her grip, crushing her hand between the T.V. and the trailer. It was very badly bruised and sprained."

"Spooky!" said Ted. "Or are we all just reading too much into all of this?" He was trying to lighten up their ghastly memories of that night.

Yolanda gave him a slightly scolding look. "We aren't reading too much into it and you know it! Debbie has been a bit like you about it all."

"The problem is, Yolanda, we can talk to each other about it all, and support each other, but at some point, sooner rather than later, I think we are going to have to put it behind us. It's just too negative."

Outwardly, Yolanda looked as if she was thinking Ted's proposal over; her arms unfolded and relaxed onto her hips. However, she had a deeper instinctive feeling that spirits from her past had been disturbed. Her mind's eye projected a black area onto her mental imagery. She didn't like this; she liked clarity. The spirits should stay within their boundaries, on the fringes of our world. Things like this, and the ominous threat to the children, placed fear where there was previously only acceptance.

"There are a few things I want to discuss tonight, just between the three of us again."

Ted looked at her. A tightness welled up in his throat, as he realized that she was accepting him as a trusted friend. In her own proud way, she wanted his help and his involvement. He felt privileged – important. "That's fine," he said, trying to sound cool and casual, "if it will help with closure."

Yolanda wasn't fooled; she knew that she had a new friend. "I think so... or, I hope that it will. It won't make malevolent spirits disappear, though, Ted. You know fine well what we all saw eleven nights ago," she insisted.

With that, Ted and Yolanda got stuck into the first ward round. They did the medication together first, to speed things up, knowing that they may well be very busy for most of the night.

One of the two new admissions to the acute wing reminded both Ted and Yolanda of Jack, the man who had just died. Jonty was also an ex-miner, who suffered with silicosis, a condition caused by the inhalation of coal dust over a long period of time. It was a terminal condition, but nowadays sufferers could live for many years, with the right treatment.

The other major concern was Valerie, a lady who, in Ted's opinion, was needing to go back to intensive care, in the main hospital wing. She had acute heart failure. Her legs wept fluid, as her circulatory system was too inefficient to draw the fluid out of her limbs. She was almost unconscious, needing constant oxygen, and her lips were cyanosed (blue, due to a lack of oxygen).

Ted went to phone the intensive care unit, and returned within three minutes. "Can you get Beth and Zoe to give us a hand, please? Valerie needs to go to 'the unit'. They have a short-term bed available at the moment."

The intensive therapy unit only had nine beds – hardly adequate to serve fifty-eight per cent of the population of Athelport and Athertown. The auxiliary hospital at Pollerwell took up some of the slack, but it was eight miles from the town centre, and had other catchment areas to worry about.

A porter and a "flying" member of the rapid response team came to escort poor Valerie up to "the unit", for the intense level of care she needed. Zoe went with them, to give a report, verbal and written, to the I.T.U. staff. About four out of five patients sent to I.T.U. would return to the wards; the less fortunate fifth person would be either transferred to other specialized facilities or, sadly, would pass away.

"What a start to the night," Yolanda stated.

She and Ted eventually took a well-earned breather with Debbie, who had been equally busy supporting their work.

"Come on, Debs," said Mother Yolanda (who was actually only six months older than Debbie), "it's coffee o'clock."

Debs reflected on her working life: "When I go to bed in the morning, I will be dreaming about blood pressure readings, E.C.G. patterns, pulse rates, respiration levels and temperatures! My own temperature will probably set the bed sheets alight and end all my bastard worries!"

Ooh, Ted thought, *Debbie sometimes swears for effect, but that is a very forceful expression for her!* He glanced at Yolanda for explanation.

Yolanda sported a cheesy grin in response. *He is getting to know us tough lasses of Athelport,* she realized. *He calls us "ladies" or "girls", but we are toughened women – except when we decide to be "ladies" or "girls" for our own advantage or amusement.*

Ted got the message: Debbie was just letting off steam.

He wanted to stay in this mainstream break-time conversation, not wishing to appear too anxious about the heavy conversation which would follow later tonight. "I will be dreaming about medication. Many of our night meds calm people or induce sleep, yet I will be woken up by dreaming about them! How mental is that?" he laughed.

The others smiled, knowingly.

Now it was Yolanda's overdue turn to chip in – and with sledgehammer subtlety. "That's quite deep, Ted. I'll still be dreaming about the man in the T.V. and his evil associates," she protested.

Debbie and Ted looked at Yolanda, in sudden realization that she had been the worst affected by the evil image they had all seen in Claire's T.V. Yolanda noticed their intense attention and felt a little uncomfortable.

"I feel like you two are getting over this quite quickly," she struck.

Debs sighed: "Well, I've already talked to you about it twice, Yol! My way of coping is to put it to the back of my mind. That doesn't mean that it's not important, or that I've forgotten about it." She was partly recapping what the friends had already discussed at length. This was mainly for Ted's benefit, to allow him a chance to catch up.

Ted had already revisited every detail of what had happened a hundred times, as, no doubt, had Yolanda and Debbie. Now was the time to have all his thoughts and conclusions proofread by his peers. These two girls were the only peers he could possibly have in this particular instance, so Ted now nervously felt that he should candidly state his position, also: "I am trying the same coping strategy as you, Debs, but when I'm alone or bored, those images, and all the related thoughts that go with them, are still hitting me hard. It's just for a few minutes, here and there, but it's still unpleasant."

"That's the first time, in nearly a year that you've been here, that you've called me Debs. Except when taking the p, of course!" She smiled and narrowed her eyes.

Yolanda nodded her approval; "It's only natural, after what we all went through less than two weeks ago."

Ted was taken aback. "So... does that mean I can call you Yol?"

"Mmm..." The Queen of 12A clearly had an important decision to make. She needed to retain some mystique, as part of her power base, but at the same time she was starting to regard Ted as a friend, as well as a colleague and, really, her boss. She was uneasy about the "short" length of time this had taken. Perhaps it was meant to be, her fatalistic side reasoned.

"I'd prefer you to call me Yolanda. Or, if you like, Mrs. Aldon," she giggled. She then continued: "That doesn't mean I'm pushing you away as a friend; it's more a male-female familiarity thing, especially when junior staff or outsiders are listening."

Ted would have normally made a witty remark at this point.

He wanted to, but Yolanda's demeanour made him realize what she was trying to maintain. *We aren't only nurses,* he realized; *we are ambassadors to each other. Common experiences bond, but diverse backgrounds and experiences require us all to conduct ourselves carefully with other work colleagues, patients and relatives.*

Yolanda, for all of her self-imposed reservation toward Ted, wanted – very rarely for her – to open up to him, with her Debs in support, her spiritual psyche. He had stood at the threshold of her private spiritual world, with his experience of this awful apparition, eleven nights ago. She knew that he was open-minded, and maybe even secretly a believer in the spirits.

"I've had spiritual experiences before, as I've already mentioned," she said. "Most have been at work, but a few unexplainable things have happened since Dad died, eight years ago next month."

The others listened in silence now, sensing that this was the right thing to do. When Yolanda noticed that Ted and Debs were genuinely riveted to her oration, it encouraged her to continue unveiling her experiences.

"If I start with experiences I've had at work, there are two main ones. About two years ago, on a winter night, a lady came on to 12A, rushed in from the cinema with acute angina. She was very frightened. The chest pain was often and severe;

she couldn't tell when it was going to strike again. That must be horrendous! The medical team got a nitro-glycerine line running, to give her continuous relief, and it worked; the angina attacks stopped very quickly. She was still very frightened of being alone, though, so I sat with her for a total of about three hours during that night, and other staff matched it. She recovered with the vaso-dilating drug therapy, reassurance and support.

"On her third night, I popped in to see her before report, and she was doing well. At 21:30, I again found time to pop into her side ward, and she was pleased to see me. We talked for about five minutes, then she said she wanted to go to the day room, to watch the news. She stood up, then suddenly turned almost blue, let out a gush of air and crashed to the floor! I screamed at the shock of her sudden collapse! I pressed the emergency call and the others called the crash team, whilst I attempted resuscitation. The team turned up and defibrillated her with the electric paddles. Then she came round – and smiled at me, as I knelt next to her. I had never seen anyone smile like that before; it had a ghostly feel to it… a ghostly afterlife feel.

"Then she said: 'You are twenty-five years younger than me. Enjoy each birthday, love, if you can…' And she arrested again.

"I cried, because this time I knew she was saying goodbye to me, and to the world. Her worn-out heart couldn't take any more.

"Why did this lady's loss upset me so much more than any other? I don't know. I just couldn't accept her death. I checked her pulse, but nothing. I checked her pupil response... nothing. I even checked her hand grip, for some sign of hope. She had held me tightly for a brief moment, and her fingers still gripped mine, but now they were lifeless. Her years had gone – just like my Nana. Just like my father, and like my brother. 'Oh, no,' I cried. I wanted her to stay; 'Please stay!' The doctor from the crash team looked at me with a disapproving scowl, and that made me realize how unprofessional I was being. I couldn't help it... I just..."

Seeing that she was welling up, Debs went over and hugged Yol. Tears filled and blurred both pairs of eyes.

"Yolly, take a break, darling. Take time out, please. You are getting in too deep again."

Ted felt his own eyes watering at Yolanda's show of empathy toward a soul leaving this Earth. To her, it was a soul as dear as any other – even those of the people she deeply loved.

As he watched in awe this vignette of love and sorrow, Ted suddenly heard his name being shouted, along the corridor from ward 14: "Ted! Ted!!!"

He sprang from his seat and raced to the outstation of ward 14. "What? What's happening?" he said, perplexed.

Beth stood there, looking horrified and pointing to the floor: "There's a cockroach!"

Beth had never seen a cockroach before, except in books, or in horror movies, where they pour out of the walls, or from the eyes and mouth of a corpse.

"Oh, bloody hell!" Ted cried, in relief. He calmly instructed: "Okay, I need a jar again. We have to report all of these creatures."

"Just kill it for me, Ted. I'm scared!" Beth pleaded.

Ted drew upon his nursing protocol. "I can't! Besides, if you crush a cockroach and it's female, the eggs will survive and spread," Ted explained.

"You are joking me!" Beth was mortified. "I thought these bugs were only from Africa, or somewhere like that, in real life!"

"They are very much here in England, too, as you can see," explained Ted. "Anyway, where the hell is Cleo? This is part of her job!"

"She's hopeless! She is only good at catching daddy-long-legs, then playing with them for two hours before the kill," Beth complained. It was true: Cleo was good at catching flyers; they were her main interest. She would stand at the window, mewing hatred at seagulls, but when it came to heavily armoured bugs, she would just swipe them with her paw, then watch as they scuttled off again.

Ted got a purpose-prepared, washed-out jam jar from the kitchen, and traced the equally perturbed cockroach to its nearby sanctuary. Sensing that it was cornered, it decided to stand defiantly, and eyeball Ted over his blocking shoe. Long antennae whipped the air around the insect's black compound eyes, while front legs protruded threateningly, like serrated spears, ready to draw anything they encountered into its hard little mandibles. Ted stooped low and, with the aid of a pencil, scooped it into the pot. *I'm so pleased insects are only small,* he thought, *otherwise we would probably never have existed.*

"Right, mate," Ted told the cockroach, partly through eccentricity, but also partly to help reduce Beth's fears, "you are on a reprieve from death row, for now, but I can't vouch for what they'll do to you in the Pathology Lab." Beth stared incredulously, not sure of what to make of this bizarre communication.

Ted spoke to her now, rather than to that vile bug: "I will have to show this to Jim in the morning. He'll inform the infection control officer – after swearing about it for ten minutes, first."

Beth calmed down now, seeing the insect captive and slightly – but only slightly – less scary. Ted was now able to talk to her gently, controlling his own annoyance at how she had worried him.

"Beth, if you see any insects or spiders in here again, please don't do that again."

"Well, what should I do?"

Ted felt the need to take this to the next level. His well-meaning novice had good potential, but she needed to learn the hard way. She needed a stark medical picture, shocking though it may be. "Beth, the last time I heard someone shout for me like that was about three months ago; it was Jen. I ran along the corridor to room 31, to find a man called Dougie standing upright, with his head slumped across his raised bedside table; his blue face lay in a pool of blood, which also drenched the bedclothes and floor. He had been dead for about half an hour."

Beth blanched. "Oh, erm, yes, I see, Ted; I see what you mean. I'm so sorry! Maybe I'm not cut out for this line of work."

Ted reassured her: "It's okay; you are doing really well here, Beth. This is a very challenging ward to be starting out on. Just take a 'note to self' about this and keep up the good work."

He suddenly realized that his reassurance might be a touch on the impersonal side. "Beth, this is a very hard job; the longer you are here, the easier things will become. You are genuinely marvellous with our elderly people; I've seen your interaction with them. That's not learnt; it's natural."

Beth didn't answer at first, so overwhelmed was she at being praised by her boss. As she put her head down, uncontrollable tears filled her eyes. "I keep thinking I'm doing well... then I think I'm crap," she sobbed.

"If you are crap," Ted said, solemnly, "then I pay my true respects to crap, dude!"

Beth looked up, greatly surprised; a senior nurse was talking to her like one of her friends would. She suddenly exploded, crying even more.

Ted's natural instinct was to go and give Beth a big, paternal hug. But he couldn't do that, and it felt cold to him to stand there and watch her cry. Perhaps further words could soothe? He waited for perhaps twenty awkward seconds, before speaking again: "Beth, we all want you to stay and work with us."

After a further ten seconds of sobbing, Beth stuttered her response: "Really? Do you mean that, Ted? I love doing this work... but I... I keep making mistakes like this."

Ted continued to reassure his new colleague: "Beth, when I

started as a student nurse, I seriously thought about packing it in probably every two weeks! Criticism after criticism got me down. What kept me going was the positive vibes from patients and peers. If you were crap, gal, I would just say nothing and let you go."

"Oh, thanks, Ted. To be honest, I've been thinking of doing something different. I love working with older people."

Ted looked at her reassuringly. "Give it a full year; you'll never look back. Now, see ya later."

Without giving her the chance to add anything, Ted returned to the main station, at the juncture of the twin wards. He was happy now that Beth was consoled, and Zoe was with her for support, as an older, experienced colleague. He would see the other girls and get them to support Beth more formally. He knew that everyone liked her, and thought that she was a natural. He felt a little guilty at being so blunt to one so young and good-hearted, but Ted assured himself that it was the only way to tell her. *Sometimes this job sucks,* he screamed inside.

Sitting down again, Ted briefly explained to his friends what had happened.

"Oh, the poor little love," Debs said.

"I know, but I couldn't just let it scuttle around the ward!" Ted rarely missed a sarcastic opportunity.

"Ha, ha, funny guy," she said, barely amused.

"Sorry," Ted continued. "Seriously, though, I feel so guilty when I have to tell her off."

"It's the only way she will learn," Yolanda said, firmly.

Then, suddenly returning to her single purpose, she said: "Shall I tell you the rest of my story?"

They had another half an hour left, before their unofficial gathering needed to be dissolved for a few hours, to do patient checks and admin. Intrigue and concentration once again now gripped Ted and Debbie, so Yolanda prepared to continue; she crossed her legs and placed linked hands across her knee, presenting formality and perhaps a symbol of self-protection.

Her story resumed:

"Once the doctor came and confirmed what I already knew, I got the lady's file, to prepare information for the G.P. and undertakers. I saw, to my amazement, that her date of birth was 29th June 1927." Yolanda looked at them both wide-eyed, recalling the scene in renewed bewilderment.

Ted, whilst intrigued, shrugged his lack of understanding, whilst Debs, obviously with the knowledge of a lifelong friend, showed a trace of surprise at the revelation.

"My birthdate is 29th June 1952!" exclaimed Yolanda, mainly for Ted's benefit. "My lady couldn't possibly have known that!"

Debbie knew the story, but as Yol told it this time, she

expressed an intense depth of emotion which sent a tingle down Deb's spine, accompanied by a strange moment of light-headedness. It was like seeing a film on the big screen, rather than at home on T.V. It was as if Debs only now realized that this had actually happened; on previous narrations she had held back a touch, and betrayed a little bit of cynicism.

Ted looked on, intently, with a more noticeable reaction than Debbie. Pinching at his now beardless chin, he was still practicing the nervous habit, days after his promise to Lucy had been kept.

Yolanda's eyes suddenly seemed to express further recollection.

"Is there more?" Ted guessed, reading her face.

With no change to her intense expression, Yolanda replied: "There *is* more! Quite a bit more."

Ted's eyes widened, in anticipation that this was only the opening phase of the story, where it would understandably have been the conclusion to many an amazing experience.

Yolanda continued: "After my lady's first close shave, I couldn't stop thinking about her shift. I went home and relaxed for a couple of hours and, helped by a little of the old grape juice, I slept for longer than normal between shifts. I dreamt of an old schoolyard, with only girls playing in it. The schoolyard was a hard surface, with high walls all around it. The entranceway to the single-storey school looked like an old Victorian railway station. Above it was inscribed the single word *'Girls'*. A huge wall, twice my height, divided the building in half."

She hesitated briefly, then continued. Completely focused now on her vision, the nurses' station, even the ward itself, no longer engaged any of her senses. She sounded monotonous, shifting into narrative:

"The girls are dressed in old-fashioned clothes – I think even before the Titanic; probably Queen Victoria times. Sorry, I always think of boat things to compare, because my dad was in the merchant navy… My dad was sunk twice in the war...

"Anyway, so the girls are playing hopscotch, kick the can, skittles, etc.; some have large metal hoops attached to rods, which they spin around the playground, constantly catching the glint of a brightly shining sun. It is a bustling, noisy scene. I walk amongst them for a while, then through the heavy iron gates in the front wall, eager to find out where I am. The school is over twice the length of the girls' enclosed play yard.

"I can now hear boys' voices, playing behind that high wall. And I am sure that I can hear my father's voice. But he had never been to school. He wasn't even in this country as a young boy. How strange!

"The school stands on a hill, with well-kept terraced houses stepped upon it. Some of the houses are large, while other streets, those farther down the hill, are more humble. The surrounding countryside is breathtaking, in early summer or early autumn. It isn't Athelport, but it feels every bit as real a place. Of all the chimneys I can see, only a single one is bellowing out smoke; I guess it is a blacksmith's forge, somewhere down there, judging by the clanking of a hammer against metal.

"Then... all of the... all of the children's voices have stopped. I go back into the schoolyard, feeling suddenly lonely, as if I've been left behind. *I've been left behind!* No one is there anymore, and I stand puzzled, alone. I must have been looking at that beautiful landscape for much longer than I realized. But the teachers can't punish me now, because I'm not from this time. I don't think I'm even from this place!

"Something white is suddenly shoved into my face. I look around, startled, to see one of the girls, smartly dressed in a charcoal-grey uniform. 'Help me chalk this out and you can join in our game,' she says, and the girl's solemn face breaks into a friendly, though limited smile. More girls are standing behind her, all waiting for me in silence. I start to chalk out the squares she wants, for our game of hopscotch. My hand trembles with excitement, but also because I can sense change approaching. I steady my left hand with my right – this is important – but, *oh, no,* the chalk dust is spoiling my clothes. I hate that! Or, do I hate that? Did I always hate dirty clothes? I don't really know; I haven't really had the chance to think about it. After a few tense minutes, I've proudly completed a pretty mean course, and now I'm feeling a sense of belonging...

"Mistiness hits me. Future doubt will be dispelled if I can map out the way; the direction in which their feet can playfully, skilfully dance. Take chalk and mark the squares: in blue chalk *39, 40, 42, 43* and *45*; in red chalk *41, 44...*

"The lead girl is smiling now. She looks friendly at first glance, but when I look over again, she seems to be wanting me to fail. But I need to fit in, by chalking out this course; I will find out whether I should be here or not. Then the girl starts to be cruel and menacing. I don't know why. Is it because she wants me to do badly and be stuck here? A long, sinewy finger suddenly protrudes and points to a mistake in my course.

"Something passes my face: a small cake of salt. The salt fractures into several pieces. *Oh, please, not another puzzle; another task I can't solve.* The chunk of salt lands in the middle of my carefully drawn squares, on square 44, its impact fading the chalk impression. A fragment bursts across square 41 and defiles it; I sob at this needless loss.

"'I'm going to say that you took that from the school pantry, when Cook trusted you to help with the chores.' I look up at this callous voice, but the face does not match the voice; a look of fear is on the girl's face.

"A strong smell of salt water, seaweed and seagull droppings swirls through the air, orchestrated by a howling wind, swept in on both borders of our scene. I can't feel the wind in my mid-position, kneeling and drawing, holding the chalk of future events. Yet, the figure that looms over me, the dominatrix, is assaulted, her face being sucked inward. The long, black hair floats in the air like a flag, blown back and forth, but resilient. Her flesh, bone and sinew cannot stand the wind; they melt, from the nose inward, as if made of plastic and having a hot poker applied. Then, with an inhuman whistling whine, her face disappears. The hair, clothing and shoes remain, like a scarecrow. I'm going to scream! I start to scream! I'm screaming!

"The other girls are still here; they now look on in fear. They watch in apprehension, as the wind builds and then howls around them. Yet, they seem not to have noticed the fate of their leader; it is no surprise. This is their charge. To each other they are nothing, nowhere and no one. Each girl produces a photo in one hand. I see a sea of faces, held firmly in caring hands, then suddenly swept away by the elements.

Each square on the game board claims thousands of pictures, of souls still here but claimed, and faded in the future.

"I see Dad amongst them, on the two red-chalked squares. He flies in the air, but then is caught in the skilful hand of an adult. He's assigned to the sea... but there's no sea here! Goat herders' bells call him in, onto rocky relief. *Why do you pick on my poor dad? He isn't here yet! He doesn't belong in this yard! Let him see for himself. Don't let my father do this now. He is not here yet. Do not disturb him now!*

"I can hear the waves of the sea against a shoreline. What?! The sea tide! The sea tide, coming in fast! It's blown by the wind – the wind which takes the future souls! The tide is coming in fast! I must be more respectful of the sea; it can hold hidden danger... dangerous currents... Too late! The waves are crashing in, suddenly, like when I will be a very young child, too far into the water at Athelport. The water sweeps me away – away from the school, where the town is gone! Worse, where is the shoreline? I can swim skilfully, but where will I swim to? Which way will take me to those souls, to the future hope that they make possible? I will swim for pleasure, but right now I swim to stay alive – or is it to *come* alive? Bright light decides the way, for darkness stops our progress, though it has its time and place.

"As I tire, the water starts to go into my mouth.

Occasionally at first, like in frightening warning, then in mouthfuls. *Oh, no!* I become terrified. The water is fresh now, no longer salty. Then it tastes awful: acidic, sweet, sickly... *Help...! Help...! Heeelllp meee!!*

"Suddenly, two strong arms pull me from what I thought was going to become my watery grave. Those strong arms of my dad have saved me before, when I was only five years old! I look up to hug and thank my daddy again, even though I feel unborn yet, in this land of aged chaos. 'Dad!' I shout. 'Dad!' But it isn't Dad. His voice is still distant, childlike beyond the heavy wall, then audible at the same time, from far out in this sea. A strong man, a survivor, still unborn as I must also be. He will save his own soul, and those of some others, yet to be. I shout and shout, but it isn't Dad...!

"Then, I see... yes, I see a small lady, in the same type of old-fashioned clothes. She has mid-brown hair, tied in a tight bun, and old fashioned, wire-framed penny spectacles adorn an elven face. A firm resolved but concerned expression pervades deeply into and beyond my own optical senses. She wears no make-up; she needs none in her role. Her skin is sallow. She wears a broad, starch-white collared, full-length dress of near black. How are her clothes dry? How are my clothes dry? No one speaks.

"The children look cautiously at me, now flecks and faint

images beaten back by the elements, behind the old French windows of the school classrooms – some imprisoned by English, others imprisoned by maths; all imprisoned by a fear of that strong, bold woman, both saviour and tormentor, who removed the challenge of their child leader's harmful ways, then rescued each and every one of them in strong, sinewy arms. I want to thank the schoolmistress. I am scared, but I approach her all the same: 'Am I safe?'

"I am safe!

"...Only about half of the crew were saved. Dad had been alone on that life-raft, with his dead, burnt friend, for nearly thirty hours. Luckily, a destroyer finally spotted him and picked him up. He never forgot the faces of those sailors, looking at him admiringly through their portholes, as he was rescued. I knew him, my bringer of life, before I even was..."

Yolanda could now hear a hissing noise in her ears. *Oh, not fresh trouble,* she silently pleaded. But it was okay; it was the hissing of the oxygen masks once more. The struggle for life goes on each day.

That medical disinfectant smell, unique to hospitals, suddenly filled her nostrils, as if she had only just come on duty and first entered the building. She looked around for several seconds, seeing only light. Then, against a bright, almost painful halo of halogen, the familiar faces of Debs and

Ted came back into focus. Kind and caring faces. *Thank goodness; they will keep me safe.*

Ted sat fascinated. He was always riveted by tales about the war, especially those of the experiences of men who had faced combat directly. Even so, he greedily waited for more. He wanted Yolanda to continue, eagerly seeking the supernatural element which would complete her account of her dad's ordeal.

Debs said: "Yolanda!" She rarely called her by her full name. "Yolanda Harrak!"

On hearing her whole name called out so formally, Yolanda was startled back to full awareness of the present. It had taken over a minute.

"Oh... so, that is one of my experiences," she mumbled.

Ted leaned slightly forward, almost sliding off of his chair; he hadn't realized that he was already perched right on the edge. "That's an amazing story, Yolanda! How can you recount your father's wartime experiences in such incredible detail?" He looked at her, awestruck. "Can you tell us any more?"

Yolanda looked puzzled. "Have I told you about my dad? To be honest, he didn't tell me very much about the war?"

"You think that wasn't very much?! That was one of the most detailed accounts I've ever heard!" Ted marvelled.

Yolanda looked at Ted as if he had two heads. "All I know

about Dad in the war is little snippets he told us: a bit about the hard conditions; about how he met Mum; and that he got sunk twice: once by a German U-boat and once by a sea mine."

Ted started to tug rapidly at his imaginary beard.

Debs interjected now, as if to help them both out, even though she was quite clearly bemused, herself.

"Yolly, you've just been telling us about your dad in the war for the last three minutes solid!"

"What?" Yolanda objected, questioningly. "Haven't I just told you about the dream I had, about the lady we lost to cardiac failure?"

"No," Debs explained, "you got partway through, then you mentioned the Titanic and got side-tracked by an amazing story about your dad in the war." She was staring at Yolanda incredulously, as she continued: "You have never told me all that about your dad before. It's fantastic to hear, but how is it a ghost story?"

Yolanda looked worried. *I've had one of those visions again,* she thought, *but this time I've also had one of those quantum experiences. Oh, shit!* She sometimes swore inwardly, but very rarely outwardly.

So, with less vision and feeling now, Yolanda quickly summarized her dream about the schoolyard and the freshwater sea. "The point is," she came to the crunch, "when the lady's only daughter came in to pay her last respects to Mum, she was, in modern guise, the schoolmistress who saved me in that dream! I had never before set eyes on her in real life. In her notes, in the social background section, brief as it was, I discovered that my lady had been a primary school teacher, in a *'long, ongoing family tradition'*. But I hadn't looked at that section of her records before I had the dream! I've now had that dream twenty to thirty times in the last two years!"

Again addressing Ted, Debbie added to the incredible quality of Yolanda's story, with which she was familiar: "Sometimes it isn't when she's asleep at home; sometimes it's a daytime vision, when we are having coffee together or I'm driving us home."

An exhausted Yolanda added, slowly and deliberately now, in contrast to her rapid speech of the last ten minutes or so: "Yeah, I suppose it's just as well I can't drive."

VI

The Isolation Hospital

Rain tapped sharply on the big old windows, sometimes lashed onto a strong, cruel wind, which heralded early signs of winter. The loud tapping became a crescendo, when accompanied by the assault on the modern Perspex skylights, and the old French windows in the conservatory.

Hedweg always felt uneasy when it was her turn to tidy this area. In daytime, in good weather, it was a warm, bright area where residents could sit and relax. Now, deserted and dimly lit as midnight approached, it had an eerie feel about it. She did her work thoroughly, but quickly; tables were sprayed and polished with cheap disinfectant, and Hedweg's eyes smarted from the spray and fumes. She felt more comfortable when the modern, familiar droning of the vacuum cleaner cut in, to stifle the sound of the wind and rain. Just a few more desolate minutes, as she mopped the floor, her back twinging slightly toward the end of the chore. She then dried the large, oblong floor area. Two yellow warning signs were planted near the two entranceways, to symbolize the completion of the task.

As soon as she had finished the cleaning, Timmy came out

of hiding from one of his myriad little cubbyholes. He charged into the middle of the floor and stood on his hind legs, offering a greeting to his human friend.

"Have you been feeding your face on za crumbs again, little man?" Hedweg returned his greeting.

Once the rain stopped, Timmy would squeeze through the seal in the old French windows. It was a gap indiscernible to the human eye, but ample to a little brown fieldmouse.

Ted was sat in the office, absent-minded and already fighting sleep, when a friendly face appeared around the door.

"I've finished the cleaning, Ted," Hedweg smiled.

Ted startled himself into full consciousness once more, and looked up at her.

"You look as if you need a nice, strong cup of coffee, young man," Heddy offered, in her slight Norwegian accent.

"I think that would be a lifesaver, Heddy," Ted replied, with a touch of irony in his voice.

As he eagerly awaited a nice, strong, milky coffee made with Heddy's good quality beans, he propped his head up with his hand, his right forearm resting firmly on the desk. *Why did I agree to do a month of nights?* Ted asked his dumb self. He knew full well that it was best to either stick to permanent day shift or permanent nights.

Ten minutes later, the soothing aroma of a caffeine-laden

beverage wafted along the corridor, to fill his nostrils and soothe his soul.

"Here you are, good sir," heralded Heddy.

"You're the only one I allow to make me a cuppa, Heddy; the others all drink dishwater," Ted commended her.

Heddy laughed. "Dishvater! Oh, Ted, you are funny, but it is true. If only you liked my black coffee; now, there is a real brew!"

Ted narrowed his eyes and smiled at her. "You are my second mum," he chortled. "Do you fancy coming onto days, so you can look after me then, as well?"

"Oh, no, sorry. I have vorked here for eight years now; you cannot teach an old hund new tricks. I have only one year and two months until my retirement."

"You will be missed," Ted lamented. He enjoyed Hedweg's Nordic precision when she explained or described things. *She uses the English language as it was meant to be,* he thought.

Ted realized it was high time to do a walkaround, then touch base with the other two carers. The precious cup of liquid accompanied him as he walked slowly, so as not to spill a single drop.

Although the building was very old, the rooms had been modernized in the past few years. They each had a one-foot square window in the door, which was handy for checking on residents without disturbing them at night. Only six of the fifteen rooms were occupied; all were ladies and gentlemen with acute mental illness. Some would go back home once their acute symptoms were treated and manageable; others, sadly, were here for a few weeks, until the psychiatrist could place them somewhere suitable. Ted peeped through room 4's window, where Peggy was fast asleep in bed. Ted was pleased.

In room 7, James was busy cautioning a suspect, before locking him up for the night. It was no use trying to get James to go to sleep when he thought he was at work; that would be "obstructing the course of justice". Ted didn't feel like being placed under arrest himself, tonight.

Three other residents were asleep; more good news. However, in room 12, banging and clanking was taking place. Ted knocked on the door and entered with permission.

"Ernie, do you want to finish that job tomorrow?"

"No, no, it's alright, son; I've got to finish it today. The wife's back from her holidays tomorrow."

Ted didn't want to ask Ernie what he was doing, because he should already know, of course! "Okay, Ernie, I'll see how you are getting on later." *That will be in fifteen minutes,* Ted secretly, silently added.

Ted approached the main dayroom, where he heard voices, which abruptly ceased as his approaching footsteps were detected. The dayroom was large, with very high old ceilings, adorned with ornate central roses around each chandelier. The coving was a work of art in alabaster. The big, almost square room was about the size of the total downstairs area of a three-bedroomed, semi-detached house. There was an entranceway at the left of the ward-side access corridor, and a double door leading out to the adjoining dining and kitchen areas. Something nice was again wafting into the room from the nearby kitchen; Mother Heddy was preparing a lovely supper for all four of them. Judy and Julie were enjoying a snack and watching a rock festival on the television.

"How's it going, *J*s?" Ted asked.

Julie smiled. "Okay. We can't get two of the guys to go to bed."

"Yes, I've noticed. There's not a lot we can do about that," Ted conceded.

Judy slouched on a recliner chair, munching crisps. She didn't even acknowledge Ted's presence, though it bothered him very little.

Heddy soon came in to warm the stony atmosphere, as much as she was able. "Supper will be ten minutes, ladies and gentlemen." She was as jovial as ever, but her eyes rolled from the direction of the slouching figure of Judy, over toward Ted. Julie noticed, but obviously sided with Heddy, for she smiled again. She smiled a lot in such circumstances.

Ted knew full well that Judy resented anyone from days coming onto nights; it meant she couldn't rule the roost as she liked to, having been on nights the longest. The senior staff nurse being here made it twice as bad. But Ted wasn't here, working nights, to be liked. Being liked was a nice bonus, but he had learnt, over the last fourteen years as a staff nurse, that more important was to be assertive. He wasn't prepared to curry favour now; to do so often led to problems.

After a delicious supper, Hedweg and Julie went to check the residents. Most needed checking half-hourly, but Ted wanted to go with them, to give support, with the two men not yet in bed. It was now twenty-five minutes since he had spoken to Ernie. They checked the sleeping residents: three were still asleep, but one, Esther, was holding a three- or four-way conversation, about a nasty man who hopped over the fence and drove off. All four of Esther's personalities eventually agreed between themselves never to go to his shop again.

Ted and Heddy went back in to see Ernie again, as Julie waited outside the room. Staff didn't generally like being on their own in these creepy old corridors and annexes. A common frightener was that someone felt a wisp of air past their ear, or through their hair. Ted would have been cynical of this, despite his past experiences, except that so many staff of all age, gender and ethnicity had given such similar accounts. Such incidents had also been reported over a long period of time. It happened occasionally on days, but frequently at night.

Ted had a theory of his own (he was prone to them): he figured the phenomenon might be more frequent at night, because there were less people around for this unexplainable energy to feed upon. He had experienced too many incidents personally, or through others, to be a dismissive non-believer now. Something that we don't understand, or can't fully perceive, is coming through to our world; he was now convinced of it.

"Ernie, I've brought Matron with me this time. She wants us all to get some rest now; it's after lights out, old buddy."

Ernie looked puzzled; "She's the matron? I thought she was the tea lady."

Ted and Heddy both tried to suppress laughter; Ernie wasn't going to be easily fooled. Ted had suffered a major reverse now, and worried about being unintentionally patronizing.

"Did you get those goldfish, son?"

"Goldfish?" Ted queried, suddenly a little wrongfooted to play fully into Ernie's enforced role-playing.

"Aye, I asked you to go and buy me some goldfish, for when I've finished this pond in the morning. Jean is coming home. She will be over the moon when she sees this."

Ted quickly twigged on. Ernie had only been here for a few days, and the staff were still trying to tune in to his stream.

"Oh, aye, I'm keeping them in the big pond, in the park, until you are ready to collect them."

"You stupid fucking arsehole!" Ernie suddenly snapped, bitterly. "The fucking cats will kill them! Or, the ducks will eat 'em! God, you are stupid!"

Ted blanched; his tried and tested strategies were floundering tonight. He and Heddy looked at each other, now knowing that Ernie wouldn't sleep for hours. They had to make sure that he didn't dismantle the washbasin and flood the room, maybe the whole corridor.

Julie had been joined in the corridor now by Judy, who had finally finished demolishing her supper.

"It's a bit depressing in that lounge on me own," Judy declared, as if the sole motive for her presence on the floor. She spoke in garbled confusion, caused by a mouthful of food.

Julie, ever cheery, and also only mildly interested in Ernie, said: "Well, there's live coverage of some good bands in a minute. Everyone's settled except Ernie."

Ted wasn't assigned to a month of night shifts without reason. The four of them would check Ernie in relays every fifteen minutes. Meanwhile, they all sat down for a while to watch the bands. Well, three of them did; Heddy got her crochet out.

After forty-five minutes, Ernie was finally running out of energy and James had fallen fast asleep. It was approaching one a.m. when the next band came on.

"I'm not keen on this group," Julie said; "I'll go and do some writing in the daily notes."

Judy got up and lumbered after her, without any explanation to Ted and Heddy.

"I'm moving her onto days for retraining," Ted told Heddy, who nodded in approval.

"I will make us a cup of coffee," offered Heddy.

"That sounds great, thank you." Ted was truly grateful.

Left alone now, he sat on a sofa, at an angle where he could see both doorways into the large, old lounge. He was enjoying the band as he kept one ear on the corridor – an old habit which hadn't left him, since those years at Atherpool General. He eagerly awaited another delicious Hedweg special, although this time he felt alert, and would enjoy savouring the drink, rather than relying on it for mere consciousness. He stretched all of his limbs and started to relax.

Suddenly, something made him sit bolt upright, as he stared at the ward-side doorway: an unearthly figure sped through that open entrance, and crossed the room at high speed! It exited the utility door, passing within three feet of Ted.

The figure was a wire-shaped outline; a hologram which could be seen through, causing a slight visual distortion as it moved. It had a wire head, about nine inches long, angled upward at sixty degrees; a matchstick-type body formed its neck and back, perhaps two feet in length. A single arm and a single leg propelled the figure in the motion of an ice skater. Its wire outline was consistently about three inches thick. The whole event lasted only a few seconds, before the figure disappeared, both physically – as it glided forty feet in a blink – and in its metaphysical presence, also.

Ted instinctively leapt up and sped after it, into the utility corridor, only to find no trace at all of the hologram form.

Strangely, he felt no initial fear at having seen it. Once it was gone, though, he no longer wanted to sit in the old lounge. It was depressing in there at the best of times; only the best T.V. in the building, and the best location to hear sounds from the bedrooms, made it attractive as a good place to sit at night.

Ted normally worked days now, and this room was fine then; it was light, busy and full of noise from several residents, when the ward was full.

Ted continued through the utility corridor, past the dining room, and followed the smell of Heddy's coffee to the main kitchen. Heddy was surprised to see him there.

"Ted, I would have brought this to you."

"I know, Heddy, but I've just seen something which has made me really uncomfortable! Something was in the lounge just now," Ted explained.

Heddy reacted to Ted's claim as if he had just said that he saw a cat out in the garden. "Oh, you have seen the spirits, Ted?" she said, matter of fact.

"I have seen something not of this world! Unless the ministry of defence is doing scientific experiments in here." He went on to describe the transparent, wraith-like figure to Hedweg in considerable detail.

"Oh," some surprise was now expressed in her voice, "that is different from what we all normally see."

"Oh, really?" said Ted.

"Yes," confirmed Hedweg, "normally we see children in various parts of the ward. Or, we see adults, sitting in rooms with real patients, or present in rooms which are empty."

Ted suddenly recalled: "Yes, I've just remembered. Almost three weeks ago I was walking with Peggy toward the dining room, when she suddenly said: 'Oh, I don't want to go in there.' 'Why not?' I challenged, and Peggy admitted: 'Because there's a little boy on the door.' I was startled. 'A little boy in the doorway?' I asked. Then Peggy became annoyed. 'No!' she said. 'There's a little boy hanging on the door!'"

"Yes, sir," Heddy agreed, "this has been happening a lot also on the nights. Remember when Steeple vas here? Little Tommy? He vas delusional, poor little soul. But, he used to say to me: 'There's little children under the floor, still alive under the fooking floorboards!' That used to frighten me, Ted!"

"It's strange hearing you swear, Heddy! But Steeple did have a vile tongue and temper! I first met him about twelve years ago, not long after I started at Atherpool General. He almost died of hypothermia in the summer," recalled Ted.

"Oh, ja!" Hedweg then likewise recollected what Ted had told her. "It vas strange for him never to learn from his mistakes, especially when he died in the middle of his eighties."

"It was in the local papers," Ted recalled; "a scandal for such an elderly man to be sleeping outdoors on a winter night. He had his own warden-controlled flat, as well."

"It was very strange, and very tragic," said Heddy, with sadness in her tone. "We should have been allowed to keep him here."

"He still had some decision-making ability, apparently," Ted reminded her. "He got too violent, as well, Heddy."

"Sometimes, but not very often," Heddy defended her Little Tommy.

"I don't know..." Ted said in a knowing, wary tone. "Once, I made him some cheese sandwiches and cut them diagonally, as I would like them. He said: 'I don't fucking want them! They're cut the wrong way! They're a parcel of fucking shite!' I thought he would calm down, and didn't have time to make any more; big mistake! He smashed his room up!"

"I know," said Heddy, "but I had a soft spot for him, you know? I tink he was always picked on because he was a small man, and a little bit odd. Like when the soldiers named him 'Steeple' because he was so short." She spoke softly, condoning the memory of Tommy.

"His surname was Seepell," Ted informed her; "it was a play on words, as well."

"Yes, it is part of your strange English sense of humour," Heddy noted, having lived in England and Scotland for almost thirty years.

Ted remembered that first night he had met Steeple, as Tommy liked to be known. Ted, Yolanda and Debbie were near the end of one of their deep sessions about the supernatural, when a rough, husky voice at the nurse's station entrance had startled all three of them:

"Hey, man! Ah came here in a fucking tank and ah can't find it now! How the fuck do ya lose a tank?!"

Ted and Yolanda had escorted Tommy back to his sideward, noticing that he had been watching a documentary about World War Two, and Arab-Israeli tanks. Tommy's psychosis provided him with a fascinating but sometimes very frightening world. He would rush up to you and excitedly inform you where to find treasure at the bottom of the sea, or how he had just flown across the English Channel in a balloon, or the best way to wrestle a grizzly bear. At other times, he would be either fleeing from danger, or barricading himself in a room – and it wasn't always his own room. He might just as likely be trying to escape from a war zone, a volcanic eruption, or trying to stop Frankenstein from getting into his house. The warning sign of his frequent attempts to abscond came when his suitcase came out from under the bed, ready to be packed. Ted remembered, sadly, his realization that Steeple was probably frightened of some media-generated threat, when he froze to death outside, two winters ago.

Heddy looked at the thoughtful Ted. "You know, Ted, he did often still get happy, or become upset because of the television set, but the spirits in this old building made his paranoia much vorse. I know this."

"There's something in what you say, definitely." Ted's hands went down to rest on his knees, as his head moved slowly and his eyes carefully scanned the air around him. Heddy looked at him with a gentle trace of concern in her normally sharp, bright-blue eyes.

The isolation hospital at Meadow Bank had been one of those late-Victorian hospital communities. Much of the original drystone walling still enclosed and mapped out the perimeter. There were five large, double-storey wards, each originally a freestanding, very long building. Most of them had been linked by what looked like post-war covered corridor pathways, to allow movement of poorly patients, without exposure to wind and rain. They were very imposing and sombre grey-slate buildings. Each had about twenty small windows on each floor, and on each face of the building; the gable ends featured only a single small window upstairs. These large buildings had all been disused and boarded up for over fifteen years now, which added to their foreboding presence. Suppressive guardians of a different era – a different world – they dominated the site during daytime; at night, you just didn't go there!

There were several administration buildings, too, each about the size of a modern bungalow. A large kitchen and refectory bisected the site, which had, at one time, been capable of feeding hundreds of people every day. This had been extensively modernized later, and it had 1960s extensions and outbuildings around it, disguising the original inner core. This area too was now closed, and at the mercy of the elements.

A powerhouse, still coal-fuelled up until the 1980s, completed the eerie scene, with its large, cylindrical, tapered brick chimney. It completed the scene, that is, with the exception of the morgue.

Dilapidated now, as were all of the other disused buildings, one could still peer through the wire mesh-barred windows from various angles. Ted had only done so once, out of sheer morbid curiosity, and then only when accompanied by Richard, the hospital's maintenance man.

"This isn't as old as most of the buildings," Richard had informed Ted. It was built at the end of the war, when most of the hospital was quickly put back into use for the influenza epidemic, and also for scarlet fever, which took a lot of children's lives.

Ted had peered through a side window. He saw an old generator, about two feet square. Next to it, well preserved, was the ghoulish "fridge" room, complete with eighteen open locker compartments, each able to hold a human corpse. It was grim testimony to the projected volume of death which accompanied all early-twentieth-century epidemics.

Richard then guided Ted around to the main focal piece: the post-mortem chamber; Ted again peered in. The hairs raised on the back of his neck, and a cold chill was sent shooting down his spine. Although parts of the roof had collapsed, a wall lined very high with white splash tiles looked almost as if it had been cleaned and polished the day before. *Those tiles aren't just to stop splashes of water,* he grimly reminded himself. A white porcelain sink contained debris, thankfully, indicating that no one had been in there recently. And there, in the centre of the small room, was the inevitable mortuary slab. It too was of matching white porcelain, and very clean looking, after all these years of disuse. It had low relief ridges formed in two sections, lining both edges of the slab – presumably, this was to prevent the body from falling off. Perhaps most ominous of all were the two holes in the slab, about the size of a domestic sink or bath's plug hole. These were positioned one at the top, for mouth fluid or cerebral autopsies; the other, in the very centre, for urine, faeces or laparotomy autopsies.

As they returned to work, Richard had displayed an expression of mild satisfaction that he made Ted feel spooked by the whole experience. Ted had seen this expression many times before, whenever Richard had the solution to a technical problem which no one else had been able to solve.

"That was interesting, but really eerie, mate," Ted admitted.

"Yeah," Richard agreed. "You never really get used to that scene, either."

"I can just picture autopsies taking place on that slab! See the scalpels at work; smell the stench of intestines and blood;

the wax-death skin being peeled aside; even bones cracking…"
Ted described it all.

"Some people see dead children on the slab, or sometimes
children standing in the narrow link corridor, between the
fridge and the autopsy room," Richard taunted Ted.

"Thanks for that, Richard, but I won't be looking again, if I
can help it," Ted said, frankly.   Ted kept to himself the
sensation he had felt whilst looking in the autopsy chamber:
that he had sensed the spirits and even the faded physical
presence of young people, lives unfulfilled and often bitter,
surrounding him in a cordon of linked hands. He felt hope; he
felt despair; he sensed despondency, caused by endless waiting,
suffering and abandonment. The restriction seemed to start at
the splash tiles, then extend outside of the building, behind Ted
and Richard. It was as if they were being forced by the spirits
of this morgue to look, to witness exactly what those lost souls
wanted them to witness. Exactly what they wanted the living
souls to experience. *Never again,* Ted promised himself. But
he knew, only too well, that in a hospital like this, that was
only wishful thinking.

Now, a couple of years later, the wiry apparition had proved
that, as the most prominent of so many such incidences.

How many hundreds – or thousands – of people had died
here, over the past one hundred and fifty years? Lives cut

tragically and very painfully short by disease. The original hospital was established here in the countryside, to isolate or at least limit outbreaks of tuberculosis, diphtheria and smallpox. Later, these vanquished diseases would be replaced by new, powerful enemies of biology; influenza and scarlet fever claimed more Britons than the two world wars combined managed to. After the wars, when people were moving around a lot more than they would usually do in peacetime, these diseases spread with ease.

Added to these physically afflicted victims were the tortured souls of the mentally ill, who had been "contained" here at other times in the hospital's morbid history, lumped together under the label of "lunatics" – until disturbingly recently, by some professionals. These were people suffering from the little-understood schizophrenia, driven to poorly treated, acute torment by voices, visions and auras. People suffering from bipolar disorders, then known as "mania" and later "manic depression", were similarly tortured by their own minds and the stimuli around them. Some were simply labelled then as "simple" or "feeble-minded". And, of course, the many who were completely sane, but who had chosen an "immoral" or "degenerate" life, abhorrent to pre-mid-1960s society; they had been sent here, too, to isolate them from "decent" society.

Ted had quivered at the magnitude, the concentration of

death and misery which had occurred within this few thousand square yards of ground. He tried to balance it in his mind with the positivity; the number of people who were also cured and saved here. Those who recovered physically or mentally, and were able to return to normal lives. It helped a little.

The saving grace of a young woman's voice brought Ted back to the present; back into a more "humane" world again:

"Ernie has finally gone to sleep," Julie informed the staff nurse.

"That's welcome news, Miss Davis," Ted replied, in mock formality, reminiscent of the times he had just been drawn back from.

"James and Peggy are both awake, though." Julie savoured telling Ted this news, in mischievous revenge.

Ted looked at her in mild despondence. "It's going to be a long, long night," he sighed.

VII

Rudiments and Ice Cream!

2009

Ted awoke to find that his hair, recently shaved to a "number four", was soaking wet. Was he ill, with a fever? *That would be a nice present to end my month on night shift,* he thought. *Bugger, there's no justice in this world!*

Then a tiny, dedicated tongue provided physical evidence to the contrary; Candy had simply decided, very thoughtfully, that Daddy needed his hair washing. Her assessment was accurate, but Ted had intended to use shampoo, under the immeasurably more hygienic setting of a hot shower.

As Ted reached up a few inches, to gently but firmly grab the tiny muzzle of the Cavalier King Charles spaniel, he heard Toby sniggering from behind Lucy's full-length, freestanding mirror.

"Wow," a sleepy Ted exclaimed, "a mirror with two real feet! What a great new invention!"

Toby's snigger evolved into a giggle, now that he had been rumbled.

"I think I will sell it to a museum or a curiosity shop, for lots of money!" Ted continued. "About ten times the amount of a little boy's pocket money!" Ted added effect by loudly rubbing his hands together, like the archetypal old miser that he was.

Toby now laughed out loud and fully lunged; advancing from behind his pavise – or big shield, as he thought of the mirror – he joined in the attack on Dad, which Candy had already started.

"Dad! I could buy a real, live spaceship for ten lots of pocket money!" Toby chuckled.

"A *real, live* one?" Ted laughed.

Adult feet rapidly ran up the stairs, toward the voices, upon the knowledge that Toby's plan – to awake the sleeping giant, with the little Ruby Cavalier's help – had worked. The heavy biped footsteps were closely followed by the slower, deliberate canter of a quadruped, which gained slowly, but still reached the scene of the action second. That would never have been the case two years earlier.

"Ha-ha!" Lucy bounded into the bedroom energetically. "Is lazy old Daddy still in bed? Just like an old bear in hibernation."

"The rudimentary requirement of doing night shift is to get plenty of sleep," Ted said, in his feigned posh accent, which he used to take the p out of Lucy and make Toby laugh even more.

"Not much hope of that on a Saturday," Lucy chortled. "Anyhoo, you belong to me again now; your night shifts are at an end. Yay!"

"Is 'Rudy-mentry' a T.V. programme for grown-ups?" enquired the innocent Toby.

"Eeeee, Tobias!" Lucy exclaimed, caught off guard. "Where do you get ideas like that from, young man?"

"From inside me head," came the reply of the six-year-old. "I think of things in me 'noodle'. That's what Dad keeps saying."

"Yes, and Dad has a soggy noodle, thanks to this little red fox of a doggy darling." He picked up Candy in both hands and held her toward the ceiling, as he still lay prone in bed. Candy licked her lips and showed the whites of her eyes in slight nervousness, but still had fair faith in her safety, as she did not tense up.

"You *have* definitely finished nights now, haven't you?" Lucy asked, with a mixture of hope and warning in her voice.

"I have indeed. You will be sick of me again by this time next week," Ted said.

"That's true. Maybe *I* should take some overtime now," she giggled.

Ted noticed faithful old Penny, now nearly fifteen, sat patiently waiting for him to get up. Ted gave her some spontaneous attention. "You are my little faithful Argos, aren't you? Without the dung and fleas." Ted playfully pulled her ears, as he had done for years, and Penny rolled over for a tummy tickle, pretending to bite Ted's fingers – as she had done for years.

"She's only playing, Dad," said Toby. "She's very gentle."

"Of course she is, Tobes; she has never bitten anyone – except little Florin's ears, when they were both pups," Ted replied.

Toby looked concerned. "Oh, why did she do that? Bad girl!"

"No, no, it was only puppy play-fighting; not real fighting," Ted assured him.

"So, she's still a good old girl," Toby smiled.

"Are we going for dinner in a couple of hours?" Lucy asked.

"That sounds like a plan." Ted was happy to. "All four of us?"

"Who knows?" Lucy rolled her eyes. "Rachael is in her room. I'll go and invite her, shall I?"

Lucy knocked on Rachael's door and heard some form of grunt, indicating acknowledgement. She entered the lair. "Hello, luv, we are going for dinner about six. Do you want to come?"

"I'm not bothered, thanks," Rachael replied, without looking up.

Lucy tried to persuade their twelve-year-old daughter; "Dad would be really pleased if you joined us. He asked me to invite you along, because he hasn't seen much of you this past month."

"Ermmm... okay, I'll go," Rachael stated, as if she were doing everyone else a big favour. "Will we be out long?"

"Don't worry; we'll only keep you from your laptop for a couple of hours," barked Lucy.

She cast a cautious but discerning eye across her daughter's bedroom floor. Its entire surface was covered with carrier bags, little piles of books, stacked between five and eight high, and cuddly toys. There was a jumble of clothing in three different clumps, almost linked together by randomly strewn socks, shoes and tights. At least three handbags – one of them Lucy's – a rucksack and a pink gym grip-bag complemented the 3D landscape, created mainly by the towers of books. About ten magazines and at least two puzzle books were concentrated in one corner, near her bed. Scribbled notes and post-its lay mainly on the outskirts of this morass. Lucy also noticed a familiar jigsaw puzzle of one of Rachael's favourite cartoons; all of the edges had been completed, but only about one-third of the scene within. It had been a Christmas present, and Lucy had seen it in its current condition on boxing day – a full four months ago! Bits of crumpled paper, thrown in temper from time to time, told their own story. How she could find her schoolbooks and homework was beyond Lucy's comprehension. Lucy looked for an upside to all of this chaos: at least there were no dirty plates and cups lying around now; the threat of stoppage to her weekly allowance had helped to cure that slovenly habit. Ah, yes, there was coral-coloured carpet in this room, Lucy was only now reminded, by a three-feet square patch near the electric wall sockets, obviously where Rachael often sat crossed-legged on her phone, reading or listening to music. It was an interesting tapestry depicting the transitional period of their daughter, into the onset of adolescence.

Lucy laughed at her abstract thoughts. *My god, I'm becoming more like Ted every day. Alarm bells!*

Then, she realized: *I'm channelling my thoughts this way to avoid losing my temper!*

She felt her lips instinctively forming shape to say: "How about tidying up a bit?" But as she thought it through, in those few moments of silence, her lips relaxed again, and her irritation was drawn back down, deep into her chest, like a dormant volcano. It would eventually erupt. *But not now,* she told herself; *keep the peace, just for tonight.* Rachael had already agreed to come to dinner, and therein lay a little victory.

"That's great, sweetie. See you downstairs at six o'clock sharp, then." Lucy planned to go out about 6:30, so gave herself a sporting chance that Rachael would be ready on time. A marginal chance!

Two and a half hours later, at 6:55, the family finally set out for dinner. Toby had tried his hardest to get a tube of sweets from the cupboard, because he was soooo hungry waiting for Rachael. Nice try, Tobes. His parents gave him a small glass of milk to tide him over.

They were eating in the village tonight, so that Ted and Lucy could have a couple of beers and glasses of wine, respectively. They had earnt it, after a long week at work. The choice of venue was not in doubt on this occasion; The Newley Arms had very recently been taken over by the Fun Factor Family Group, and Toby was very keen to get into the soft-play area.

Whilst Ted, Lucy and Rachael studied the menu, Toby jumped up and down in impatient excitement. "Mum, Dad, can I go in and play now? I want to play."

"You have ants in your pants, Tobes," said Ted.

"Yes! I need to get into the soft-play to bash them out of my pants!"

Everyone laughed at Toby's clever answer, including a few customers at nearby tables. Tobes wasn't exactly communicating quietly; shouting mode was in play! Toby was very small, and people often thought him to be younger than his actual age; this often made his witty comments even funnier and cleverer to observers. But the unexpected attention of others made him a little self-conscious, and he calmed down a fair bit.

"You are going to leave me behind, Mr. Tobias," Rachael predicted. She then turned to her parents; "Can I have a veggie burger with salad and fries, please?"

"Well, Toby, choose your meal, then you can go and sign in," Lucy told him.

"Fish fingers, chips and beanzzzz, pleeezze," Toby rhymed, as quickly as possible.

"Okay, then, see the man to sign you in, but straight out when dinner comes." Lucy had Toby quite well-disciplined.

Toby leapt up to the station at the entrance of the soft-play area.

"Hello, I'm Jonathan. Shall I sign you in?" a kindly, gentle-spoken young man enquired. Toby liked his yellow t-shirt, with lots of smiling soft-play balls all over it: red, blue, yellow and green. He went shy for a few seconds, then nodded, mesmerized by the t-shirt.

"I think you are clever enough to sign your own full name on this form. Then you get a wristband with your own special number on it!"

Jonathan gave Toby a pen and reached into the nearby cupboard for a wristband. Turning back to Toby after about twelve seconds, he was taken aback when he saw Toby's entry on the form:

"Tobias Edward Fry, esq."

"Wow," Jonathan exclaimed, "what a clever lad!"

Toby was too excited and impatient to take much else in, other than his beloved new play area. Two other boys were in the central ball tower, to where Toby was first drawn. To Jonathan's surprise, and some unease, Toby only interacted with them very briefly, perhaps about two minutes; for the remaining twenty minutes or so, before he was called out by his parents for dinner, he seemed happy running around, throwing the coloured balls at an imaginary friend... or enemy, Jonathan intensely noted.

Meanwhile, Lucy and Ted had an opportunity to catch up with each other, and what Rachael had been doing of late. Their daughter was just at the cusp of becoming a teenager, at twelve years and nine months of age. She was a quiet, studious girl, who enjoyed her own company and, occasionally, time with her friend in deep conversation. Her dad was proud that her head was always in a book, or that she was always investigating something on the internet. "She's a chip off the old block," Ted would often boast.

Lucy held a different perspective. She was pleased that Rachael was studious and doing well in most subjects at school but, on the other hand, she was also concerned that she wasn't socializing enough, not even with her own family, and certainly not with her peer group.

"What are you into at the moment, Rach?" asked Ted.

Ted was seated opposite Lucy, and Rachael to her mother's left; it was boys on one side of the table and girls on the other, and Ted's ally had abandoned him!

Rachael stopped staring down at the red tablecloth, and looked across at an angle, at her questioning father, flicking back her long, chestnut ponytail, in a gesture that she was now paying attention.

"Erm... what am I into? Can you be more specific, Dad?"

"Ah, sorry." Ted realized how vaguely assumptive his question had been. "I was meaning your school studies, or just your reading and surfing in general."

Rachael was willing to talk about her history studies with

her dad, but not, at this confusing time, about a lot of other, more personal stuff.

"The Wars of the Roses at school, Richard of York, Warwick the Kingmaker and Edward IV. It's great! And I've been reading about Catherine de Medici at home. What a bitch!"

"She was that! She tore France apart for decades," Ted smiled, thoughtfully. His steel-blue eyes were animated now, with intense interest in this late medieval and Renaissance history. "What about Richard III?"

"We haven't got that far yet; just up to where Warwick put a feeble Henry VI back on the throne in 1471."

"Ah, yes," Ted recalled, "poor old Henry; he was just a puppet in the hands of the great lords. Do you think that Warwick—?"

"Ooh, here's dinner coming!" Lucy interjected. She liked history, too, but not to the geeky extent that Ted and now Rachael could sometimes take it.

Ted went to collect Toby for a break from his plastic and fabric world of exploration. "Toby, come and check out for a few minutes. Toby! TOBEEE!!" He called his boy for a good forty-five seconds. After a whole minute, which felt more like ten to Ted, Toby emerged, lathered in sweat and ever so excited. He had been in there for a good twenty minutes, and

Ted was surprised to see that his energy didn't seem to have been diminished at all in that time.

"Toby," a relieved Ted exclaimed, "I thought you had been eaten by a big plastic monster ball... or maybe an angry space-hopper!"

Toby was too distracted by excitement to laugh at Dad's banter, as he normally would have done. "Dad, Dad, I've made a new friend!"

"That's great, Tobes. Tell us all about it over your fish fingers, chips and beans," Ted advised.

They dashed to the dining area, Toby in manic excitement and Ted wanting to eat a nice, hot main course.

"Oh, Toby!" Lucy cried out. "You are soaked right through with sweat! Sit down for a bit and try to calm down, darling."

"I can't stay for long, Mum. I want to get back to play and talk with my new friend," objected Toby.

"That's not a problem," Lucy reassured the still panting boy. "Have something to eat, then you can go back." She took his hand and brought him close to her, him still standing, she sitting. She guided him gently by both shoulders, calming him with a gentle massage of his shoulders and neck. She was dressed practically for the occasion, so his damp hair and clothing did not present a problem, as she held him closely.

"Well, Toby, what's this amazing new friend like?" Rachael

said, with interest, but also to support her Mum in calming her little brother.

"Rachie, I need to eat my dinner and get back."

Rachael looked a little non-plussed, as well as amused. Ted and Lucy tried not to laugh at this cute sibling interaction, because they wanted Toby to eat most of his food. This was often a bold objective at home; tonight, it would be easier to find a wild giraffe in Antarctica! Nonetheless, they always had to try, so serious faces and little convo were known to be the best recipe for success on this one. Lucy had soothed him considerably, and he went around to sit next to his beckoning dad.

"A bit of everything," Ted warned him.

Not a minute later, a little voice piped up once more: "There, Dad, I had a fish finger, a chip and a bean."

Ted despaired at the sarcasm, and ran his fingers through his hair, clenching it between them in concealed exasperation. Through quick thinking, he tried to amend the problem: "Well, Tobes, you can't leave the other fingers, chips and beans out; they will get upset." His tone was joking, but for purpose this time.

Toby remained quiet, eating as slowly as he could get away with. A minute later came his gambit. "Look, I've eaten nearly all of it," he convinced himself, and hopefully his parents, as well.

Ted and Lucy looked at the plate, with almost half of the food still on it. They couldn't help but notice that the floor in Tobias's vicinity had become an ocean hotbed, a breeding ground for the fish finger and chip. They were already multiplying, it seemed, laying small orange eggs not dissimilar in appearance from the common baked bean, which so many humans usually eat. They looked at each other and, as experienced parents, they came to the same conclusion: non-verbally, they agreed that Toby could go back now. Hard work would have to be put in, over a period of time, to reduce this sporadic eating problem.

"Okay, Tobias," Lucy took the lead through subconscious agreement, "off you go, but take it easy or you'll be sick."

In seconds, Toby had gone.

"We'll have to clean that up," said a conscientious, embarrassed mum.

"I'm onto it," said Ted, sporting a small wad of serviettes. "I'm not even going to look in that plant pot behind his chair!"

A large, ornate, Mediterranean-style pot, themed tastefully in blues and yellows, stood dutifully on the broad windowsill, directly behind Toby's vacant dining chair. It contained an infant cheese plant, which would either become a monster from all the extra nutrients it was receiving, or, equally as likely, would wither and die from absorbing too much salt and additives. The next few weeks would decide the mute plant's fate.

"Oh, go on. I dare you to take a peek," Lucy challenged him, needing a touch of light relief.

Ted peered over the broad terracotta rim. "I hope those fish fingers are amphibian," he mused; "they have laid at least ten eggs in here!"

Lucy and Rachael smiled. Rachael was enjoying the zany antics of her parents tonight; at other times they could be a drag, and a bit of an embarrassment.

"He's always keen to get back to soft-play," Lucy noted, "but tonight he actually seems desperate."

"He's coming to that age of huge adventure and imagination – lucky lad," replied Ted.

Lucy responded: "God help us all, if he has an imagination anything like yours!"

Lucy, Ted and even Rachael laughed heartily at this.

The meals were still just warm enough to enjoy, and Ted continued to savour his chicken Marengo. It was slightly dry, but the sauce and supporting vegetables – petit pois, French green beans and sautéed potatoes – were magnifique! Lucy was critically happy with her steak in Béarnaise sauce, and the same veg as Ted. She picked at it, but ate almost half, which testified to an adequate fare, in her case. Rachael's meal was polished off in quick time; she hadn't eaten since breakfast of two Weetabix.

Plates were returned to the attentive waiter, but no meaningful conversation had resumed, before a very upset Toby came careering back to their side, this time accompanied by a rather worried looking Jonathan.

"I'm sorry, Mr. Fry," Jonathan apologized, "but I've had to bring Tobias out of the soft-play area."

"Whatever for?" asked an alarmed Lucy.

"Well... erm... Toby went back into the soft-play area full of happiness. He played fine on his own for a few minutes, but then he started to shout and cry. I had to bring him out – sorry."

"I think he has just got himself overexcited," Lucy rationalized. "Thanks for monitoring him so well. We'll soon sort this out with some ice cream."

"Oh, yes, that should help him," Jonathan said, forcing a smile. He went back to his desk, still looking concerned about Toby.

"Toby," Lucy continued, "we were just about to order dessert, and I know a big boy who would love a nice Fun Factor Ice Cream Bonanza! Do you know him?"

Toby continued to sob, yet managed a pro-ice cream nod

amongst a wash of salty tears, and now a runny nose. Serviettes were proving to be a lifesaver tonight, and Lucy started to fight back the salty deluge, concentrating mainly on the nose, of course.

"That's better! So... who is that lucky little boy, do you think?"

"I hope that's... that (sob) is me... Tobias... (sob) Edward... F-Fry."

"That's right, Mister Toby Tedward Pie!" Ted intervened, to help cheer up the unhappy little man.

Lucy looked at Ted with just a hint of "don't interfere" in her eyes. Ted could sometimes work wonders with Toby, but her maternal intuition told her that abstract humour was misplaced at this current moment in time. There was no contradiction, though; unity between parents was another golden rule when dealing with the Tobe-tantrum. But, Ted noted the slight flair in his wife's nostrils; even a cute little ski-slope nose could betray irritation, he knew.

Lucy now cast the line of logic a little farther out, in a bid to finally reel in her son's unhappiness and, hopefully, restore order to the outing. "That's him. But, there's one thing wrong with this picture..." she drew an imaginary frame around Toby's face: "big boys don't get this upset about soft-play, do they?"

Toby gradually rallied, especially when a boy and girl bounced past with their ice cream feasts. The brief snotty siege to Toby's nose had ended now, and their candy-laden feasts had a dramatic effect on his sense of smell. Then he spotted their mounds of ice cream, held tightly as if they were the Crown Jewels, encrusted in all types of chocolate, mallows and brightly coloured candy pieces. Well-honed mum Lucy saw the opportunity to get Toby back onto an even keel, with the magic that was ice cream. After a few minutes of indulgence, Toby was his old buoyant self again. The silently expectant cheese plant received no extra nutrients, and its amphibian eggs were spared the threat of being frozen out of their cosy incubation.

Now, as empty plates of treacle toffee pudding, New York lemon cheesecake and ice cream clattered, one by one, against the table, the family thought about going home. A fourth plate was not empty, though; half-nibbled crusts, chunks of pastry-clad apple and melted ice cream indicated that Lucy had ordered then picked at apple pie with ice cream.

Ted took up the parental torch again now, as cheerful Toby was more his ticket. Yet, he also had some investigating to do, before he was satisfied that something strange or unpleasant hadn't befallen his son. Just for a couple of minutes, before they left, he needed to carefully ask Toby a few questions. He knew that Lucy wanted this, too.

"Did you enjoy that, Tobes?" he asked.

"I did, Dad, I did!" he enthused.

"Did you enjoy the soft-play area, when your friend was there?" Ted continued.

"He was great fun. He is very clever, too!" Toby said, admiringly.

"Was he? Tell us a bit more about him," invited Ted.

Toby was eager to talk about his new instant idol. "He was an older boy with a fancy-dress costume on. He did tricks! He did somersaults and handstands, and he could go away and come back again; he did it to make me laugh!" Toby then got the giggles, which then soon escalated into an out of control, almost shouting bout of strange laughter.

Ted touched the boy's shoulder. He detected increasing perspiration, once more. "That sounds very interesting, Tobes. What an extraordinary lad he must be! Try to stay calm whilst we are at the dining table, mate," Ted advised.

Lucy intervened now, as a few seconds of stalling silence occurred: "Yes, Toby, don't start getting too excited again. It's enough for one day."

"Why did he leave at the end, when it made you sad?" Ted was using his professional skills now, to try to find out why Toby had been so upset.

"He left lots of times, then came back again," Toby said, wondering why his mum and dad didn't understand. This friend was special. He was a special magic boy!

"He kept hiding?"

"No, Dad, I just told you: he kept disappeawing and reappeawing. He didn't have to go away to do it, coz he is magic! It was a bit scary, then funny!"

"Did he do anything else?" Lucy asked.

"He put the balls in his ear to hide them. Up his nose, too," Toby said, admiringly.

Ted and Lucy couldn't help but look at each other. Toby could, on occasion, get carried away with his fantastic stories. Ted cautiously probed further: "What kind of fancy dress was he wearing, Tobes?"

Toby thought hard, as an index finger rose and lodged itself in the gap in his teeth – or, rather, one of the many gaps in his teeth, as a six-year-old tends to have. "It was before people had cars, but not Napoleon times." Ted was always reading stories to Toby about Napoleon, Joan of Arc and Alexander the Great. That, or the marvellous worlds of Greek and Norse mythology.

"After Napoleon, you think?"

"Sort of Queen Victoria times, like on my film wiv chimney sweeps. He could make himself young and old, young and old.

I didn't like that trick, so he stopped doing it."

"Okay." Ted now spoke with a touch of concern: "Was he going to a fancy-dress party?"

"No, he said he was going back to the hospital on the hill, to have a rest."

Ted now felt a sudden tingle down his spine. He didn't tell Toby much about work, with him still being so young. "Did he look ill, Toby?" asked Ted.

He noticed a slightly disapproving glance directed at him from Lucy, as if the questioning had gone far enough. However, Ted knew that it was now or never, for he didn't want to be dragging this experience back up again with Toby, after tonight. But Toby was actually still quite happy to talk – even to boast – about his new friend.

"Erm... I don't know. He was thin. He was here because he had been poorly, and was going to the hospital on the hill for some rest – that one where you work, Dad. Ooh, you might see him at work!" Excitable energy suddenly returned to Toby's mind and body.

"I might," Ted agreed, humouring Toby, "but Dad mainly looks after old people."

"The boy will be hiding in the trees. He's clever; he hides in the trees so they can't take him away. When he didn't hide, the people with the old clothes took him away from his poorly mum. He came back and his mum had gone forever! Now, he hides from the people with new clothes. They can't take him away because he is so clever now; he will hide and hide and hide until his mum comes back again! He said forever can't last forever!"

Lucy had heard enough for now. "Toby, is your imagination running away with you again?" She used this expression often, with her excitable lad.

"No, Mum! He was real, then he went away," Toby lamented.

"You mean... he said he was going home?" Lucy second-guessed.

"He said he was going to the hospital. Then he faded away; I waved to him. He was special. He didn't need to walk around like we do; only when he wanted to play," Toby explained.

Lucy was lost for words. She and Ted both wanted to ask Toby why he wasn't frightened by what he had seen, but they knew that they couldn't do that directly. Ted also noted that Toby was giving a very articulate description of what had been said; there was no way this could be the imagination of a six-year-old, even his clever boy!

Rachael whispered in her mum's ear: "Mum, this is freaking me out! I'm going to the lav, then home." She sensed Toby's disturbingly adult wording, as her dad had done.

"We are all going home now, darling. Just meet us at the door in five, please," Lucy told her.

Rachael nodded glibly and trotted off.

"I'm just going to pay the man at the soft-play desk," Ted smiled; "I'll catch up with you in a minute."

Lucy twigged, instantly. "Okay, Dad, we'll see you on the way up the hill, in a minute. Come with me, Tobes."

The soft-play was free if your family were here for a meal, but Toby didn't know that. Ted could quickly do a bit of baseline detective work, by asking Jonathan what had happened.

"Hi, there. Can I just ask what happened? What you saw just now, when Toby got upset?"

"Certainly." Jonathan was happy to be able to help. "Is he okay now?"

"Oh, yes. Ice cream was the perfect remedy." Ted forced a grin. Jonathan gave a tired grin in return.

"Your son was playing quite happily on his own before his meal. He briefly interacted with two boys, who came in together, then he was preoccupied on his own, mainly with his own games and characters."

"Does that sort of play happen often?" Ted asked.

"Not really, but there are some kids with much greater

imagination than others; soft-play often brings that out in clever children, I've noticed," explained Jonathan.

"Thanks for that," said Ted. "Did you notice him when he first got upset, and you had to bring him out?"

Jonathan's eyes steered away for a second and, not unnoticed by Ted, he nervously sniffed a couple of times, as he considered his reply. The awkward pause lasted a few seconds. Eventually, he answered:

"Erm… it looked as if he was asking someone imaginary not to leave. He seemed to be grabbing at them and keeping a hold on thin air. Then, it seemed that he was being pushed himself – not quite falling, but being forced backward. There was definitely no one there with him. But I have to say, Mr. Fry, that it was very clever solo play, though I did think it a bit strange for a six-year-old. He doesn't go to a special drama school or anything, does he?"

Ted was too concerned to smile at the question. "Oh, no, he goes to Cilchester Primary. Who else was playing in the ball tower at the time?"

"Two girls had started to play on the climbing frames and obstacle course; the other two boys, who have gone now, were playing completely separately from Toby. I hope you don't mind my saying this, Mr. Fry, but those boys seemed to be carefully avoiding him – as he was them."

Ted noticed that this area was completely separate from the soft-play ball tower; it seemed to be aimed at older kids, and the two girls were about nine or maybe ten years old.

He sighed; "It's strange, indeed. Well, thanks for putting up with my interrogation, Jonathan; it's appreciated," Ted said.

"It's fine. I feel a bit better for explaining, to be honest. Like you, I find it a bit strange."

"Okay, take care," Ted said, as he departed.

A bit strange? Ted pondered. *It's a lot strange!* Poor Jonathan was clearly genuinely concerned, and he had been very helpful.

As he departed, he heard a slightly belated cordial goodbye from Jonathan: "Thanks, sir. Come back soon."

Jonathan, in fact, felt a little guilty that he could not tell Ted that he had seen this happen twice before, in the brief five weeks since the soft-play area had opened.

Company policy and protocol did not allow him to disclose information about other customers' experiences, he comforted himself.

He checked in the register, which was still the first book since soft-play had commenced. He was eager to find the details of the other two children, whom he considered to have had as equally bizarre a visit as poor Toby had just had. He roughly remembered the dates, as he flicked through the ringbound pages. He found the first quite quickly; it was last Thursday, at almost exactly the same time. Again, the child in this case, at only five years old, had entered his name in full, in amazingly good handwriting, almost calligraphy, as was Toby's.

Jonathan's hand trembled slightly now, as he scanned for the second suspicious entry he sought. He flicked the pages, his eyes moving rapidly down the rows of text. Line after line of childlike writing zipped past his eyes, and then... *"Sarah Anne Marie Brentburn"* – another perfectly written full name graced the register.

Or, he started to wonder, was it cursing the register?

Just a minute!

His jaw dropped what felt like a mile. He actually felt twitching, followed by aching in his lower jaw, as if he were over-chewing something. His eyes now changed axis, moving slowly across the register...

Ohh! Oh, shit!

It was one of his duty days, but Jade was covering soft-play that evening.

He pawed his way through to the next Thursday... dreading... mistrusting and hating his thoughts.

Oh, no...

Oh, bloody hell!

He felt suddenly as if his mind were in a vice, being squeezed to implosion, concentrated to a point where the neurons would destroy each other in a deluge of electrical overload. *Get the fuck out of it...*

This was happening to a child every Thursday evening, each time just after seven p.m. Five weeks; five Thursdays; five calligraphic signatures; five hysterical children! He himself had endured three of these events; he would have to check with Jade what had happened on her night. Hopefully nothing, then the problem would be diluted, perhaps. Then there was Belle, short for Isabelle, named by nearly all of the staff "Isa-hell", though only in her absence. The last e was silent, of course. Belle was the assistant manager, whom Jonathan disliked as much as all the others did. He repeatedly told her that he didn't like being called Jonny, and she responded by now always calling him Jack – unless the owner was present. Maybe Jade could ask her on his behalf; "Jonny" certainly wasn't going to ask her – no way!

Roll on nine-thirty, he dreamed. *I can get off once I've cleared the kids out at nine, tidied up and done safety checks. I need a few cans and a spliff!*

Four figures toiled up the steep bank, headed for home. The

wind had increased, making the crisp winter evening a cruel challenge. Scarves were drawn up and hoods tightened, to reduce the biting of exposed skin. There was little place for conversation, all breath being consumed by effort, creating funnels of vapour above each covered head; there would be plenty to talk about once they reached home. When a red, plastic ball fell out of Toby's trouser pocket, and blew down the hill as far as the library, in a few seconds, Lucy scowled in annoyance.

The welcome sight of their three-bedroomed semi offered flat ground at last, after that steep, wind-bleached climb. As the four negotiated the small porch, which doubled as an overburdened cloakroom and shoe cupboard, Ted was ever the gentleman, waiting in the cold whilst his kids and wife got unwrapped and into their slippers.

Lucy then took Toby to one side, while Rachael made herself a drink, before being sucked away by an irresistible magnetic force, which pulled her straight upstairs to her bedroom. She had at least offered a magnanimous "Thanks, Mum and Dad, for a nice meal," as she removed her coat. Rachael would probably not be seen again until 8:25 the next morning, when she would shuffle around, grumbling and moaning to no one but the two dogs. Getting up at 8:25 allowed her a whole fifteen minutes to get ready for school.

She was still just at the pre-preening age; in a year's time she would have to be up at 7:15, to carry out a prolonged routine before she could possibly leave the house.

Tobes also had school tomorrow, but a little gentle interview was required by both parents: Lucy over the practical and Ted the spiritual. Lucy could be, and was, more direct.

"Toby, why did you have a soft-play ball in your pocket?"

Toby glanced from side to side, clearly reluctant to answer.

"Toby, look at me and tell me the truth, please. I'm not angry with you; you already know that you have done something that is wrong."

"I know, Mummy, I know," he said, starting to nervously fidget.

"Just relax, Toby. Remember, we always need to be open with each other," Lucy persuaded the boy.

"I know, Mum, but I'm worried you might think I'm silly," Toby almost whispered.

"Try me, Toby," challenged Lucy. "I don't think I will think you're silly. I hope not."

"My friend gave it to me," Toby almost whispered, as if he were giving away a secret.

"Tell me everything, please," Lucy said, indulging the whispering.

"He said I need it for *life*," Toby spoke louder now, in a

declaration which sounded as if it were being read straight from a politician's speech.

"What?" Lucy and Ted were both a little taken aback.

"I need it for *life*. Red ball for life; yellow ball for poorly; blue ball for cold and hungry," explained Toby.

"Your... your friend told you that?" Lucy tried to sound confident before Tobias, but inexplicable terror was starting to surge within her stomach.

"Yes, Mummy, honest. He was a clever boy. He was from the olden days – that's why he was so clever."

Lucy looked at Ted, and received an unexpected look in return: Ted looked troubled. Lucy turned back to Toby; "Okay, sweetheart. What a day, eh? Let's get you a nice drink of milk before bed. Chocolate or banana?"

"Banana for your monkey, please," laughed Tobias.

Lucy laughed too, as she scooped him up. "Oh, what a heavy monkey you are becoming," she smiled.

Toby was soon tucked up in bed. Lucy sat with him for about ten minutes, to make sure he was okay, but he seemed completely unfazed by the evening's events, and was soon fast asleep, his milk only half-consumed.

Lucy was, unsurprisingly, very eager to touch base with Ted, over what the man at soft-play had said. Ted knew this full well, and he wanted to talk, too. He cracked open a bottle of lager to calm him, as he waited for his anxious wife's return. Supping from the bottle, as his mind wandered, he suddenly felt cold, wet fluid trickling down his neck, marking one of his best white shirts with pale, brown lager. *Bugger!* What a mess... in more ways than one!

After ten minutes, happy that Tobes was well settled, Lucy came back downstairs, looking slightly more composed than Ted had expected. She sat down at a right angle to Ted, who usually lounged on the sofa, but was on the edge of his seat at present. She sat forward in her chair, hands clenched together in front of her, between denim-clad knees, which moved rapidly back and forth about an inch, with each movement. She wasn't as calm as she first appeared, Ted realized.

"Do you want to fill me in, Ted?" she asked.

Normally, that would be a big open for a wisecrack, but tonight Ted was also in a serious mood; a very concerned mood. The spirits were apparently now affecting his family.

"I sure will. It seems that Toby was playing with an imaginary friend in the soft-play ball tower. I got the impression, from what Jonathan said, that—"

"Jonathan?" enquired Lucy.

"The young guy who was running the soft-play tonight. He brought Toby back when he got upset," explained Ted.

"Ah, yes. He seemed very concerned," Lucy observed.

"Is this a listening or an interrupting conversation?" Ted was starting to grow irritated.

"Sorry, hun, I'm listening," she apologized, knowing that this was a sign Ted was also rather stressed by the evening's events.

"So... erm... oh, yes," a tiring Ted got back on track, "he said Toby looked to be carrying out role-play with this imaginary friend; it sounded quite bizarre! Combined with all that Toby told us himself, something strange seems to have occurred, don't you think?"

Lucy pondered, her worried, disturbed eyes as beautiful now in adversity, Ted thought, as they were in happiness and love. Very deep brown, they looked up from a despondent gaze at the floor, to engage Ted's eyes with a look of need: the need to make sense of this, and for Ted to help her in their journey.

She saw a tint of despair in Ted's steely, mid-blue eyes, but she was also fortified by the look of experience and resolve. Most importantly, she saw deep and long-lasting love for her. It helped straight away, and gave her some of the comfort and strength that she needed more and more, lately.

"What do you think, darls?" Ted spoke again, just before his wife was ready to ask him the same question. *Intuitive, strong man,* she thought.

She rubbed her forehead, then tapped it twice with the flat of her hand. *Come on, Lucy, cope with this like you cope with almost every problem. Bring back order and common sense, you daft mare!*

Ted had an unforgivable abstract thought in such an adverse moment: Yolanda was left-handed, too. *Rare women bless me,* he thought.

"You know me well enough, great Bear. I have to find a rational explanation for everything… especially this shit!" her voice searched, rather than stated.

"Of course," Ted concurred; "this is our son this time. But where do we start?"

"I don't want you to get annoyed or frustrated, Ted, but can I just start clearing some shit to one side, to help us understand?" Lucy was recovering her old acumen for common sense now; for the creation and maintenance of order.

"Yeah. I think I know what you are going to ask me, anyway. Come on, then," a wary Ted beckoned Lucy.

"Have you been telling Toby about your ghost stories, or aliens, or even innocently about strange things at the hospital?" Lucy probed, without accusation in her tone.

"Absolutely not; no way! He's far too young. I only started telling Rachael anything like that about a year ago," Ted objected.

"Rachael! Could she be telling him stories?" Lucy

exclaimed.

"I very much doubt it; you know how protective she is toward Toby, because of the age difference and because of his disadvantages. She's his mother-hen big sis!" Ted attested for his daughter.

"I know," Lucy resigned. "So where is this coming from? I hope he doesn't have a mental disorder, on top of his autistic traits! My poor little boy doesn't deserve that." She started to sound despondent.

"Come here, youuu…" They both stood up as one, and Ted hugged Lucy close to his chest. He was able to kiss the top of her head, due to the seven-inch difference in their heights. Then, he gently combed back her hair and kissed her on the lips, using his cheeks to gently sweep the tears from her cheeks. As they hugged, she relaxed. He stroked her small back with his wide reach. "My little Willow," he said, tenderly.

Ted really and truly wanted to draw Lucy into the world of spirits, even just as an open-minded member, as he himself was. But he knew that he couldn't, because of her down to earth values.

The other problem was that it now related directly to a member of their immediate family: their vulnerable son. No, Ted realized, he would have to play this down for now.

"It's probably just Tobes's imagination, Willow, running wild; running free, as always." Ted almost physically bit his lip, for telling his beloved something he really didn't believe to be the case.

Surprised, but now beginning to tire, Lucy warily accepted Ted's conclusions – for now. She'd had enough for one night, especially when she had poor control of her environment. "Ah, well," she suggested, "shall we watch a quick film before hitting the sack?"

"Yes," Ted agreed, "let's leave this for a while; it's insoluble at the moment. We need some downtime, before both of our brains go on strike."

They snuggled up on the sofa.

Neither of them had seen the film before, and neither would have a clue how it ended; they were both fast asleep before halfway. When Ted awoke, Lucy had gone to bed before him, having risen first, and unable to stir her snoring hubby.

Ted had been longing to tell Lucy his real theory on what was happening, but he couldn't. It was time to start doing some solo groundwork, first.

The problem was – if it could be seen as a problem – that some people are sensitive to the spirits, and others, probably the vast majority, he reasoned, aren't. Ted didn't believe in ghosts, as such, but he now had behind him too many unexplainable encounters, which lay beyond the dimensions of the physical world. And it appeared that Toby was already sensing this "sixth dimension", for want of a better word. A dimension which tormented, teased and confused the rules of our known world, through our own five senses – especially sight, touch and sound.

Ted could not fully expel the cerebral imprint of the wire wraith he had seen recently; *Oh, that was only two weeks ago!* Why had he seen it yet felt no fear? None at all? Perhaps it takes half a lifetime of exposure to accept. He was forty-four years old now, and all of his previous "incidents" had caused him apprehension and fear – yet, the most physical experience of all hadn't. This gave hope, if not understanding.

Ted felt compelled to go outside; he wanted to look up at the stars – for an answer? No, their beauty and the sheer expanse invoked a million questions, but not a single answer was to be found out there in the void, the overpowering void of space. Yet, how he loved it so!

Ted felt strangely close to Yolanda, in this moment of engulfing awe. She was of the stars as much as she was of this world. The Moorish lady's experiences far transcended his own, but he understood her a little more with each supernatural event. Her lineage was imbued with ancient tradition, which heightened her perception of the spirits. She had been able to experience her own father's wartime suffering vividly, without any actual detailed knowledge of what he had been through! What else did she know, without consciously knowing it?

Yolanda had retired last year, aged sixty. Ted still had her address, and he still had her phone number. It comforted him that he could contact her, but only if the need really arose.

Not quite yet, he told himself; *it's not quite time to beckon help from Avalon.*

VIII

The Kettle of Cidre

Yolanda, if this doesn't work, I'll have to contact you for advice, Ted resolved, with stored courage. He remembered his military strategy: always keep some of your forces in reserve – if possible, the best. Ted told himself that he was doing that. But he was disguising the fact that, though he hankered for contact and support from Yolanda, he was also shitting himself about it, too! Pandora's box could well be flung open, to curse his world once more, physically, spiritually... and personally.

Ted was taking the precaution of travelling to meet Jonathan in a taxi; he was bound to want more than just one pint, once he got settled in the pub. He also didn't want the young man to know his car and registration at this point. They had agreed to meet on a Tuesday, as the pub would probably have a quiet corner, where they could talk in reasonable private.

Two weeks earlier, Ted had gone back down to The Newley Arms, to surreptitiously see Jonathan about Toby. Jonathan was the last member of staff on duty in the pub, as Ted had hoped; he was washing the used glasses under the spinning water jets, above the bar's sink. He had looked up from his thankless chore, greatly surprised to see Ted frequenting the place again.

It was his own penultimate night there; his questioning and investigating had cost him his job! A transfer had been offered to him, to keep the peace. Jonathan had dutifully explained to an enquiring Ted that he wasn't supposed to discuss details involving other clients, but Ted had, with relative ease, persuaded Jonathan to meet him and discuss it in private. Both men were, on balance, equally eager to get this strange phenomenon off their chests.

Jonathan lived two miles from Cilchester, on the new farm road. A nice little country pub nearby was the agreed rendezvous.

"Just here please, Mike," Ted pointed to the quiet pub.

"Ah," exclaimed Mike, "funny how, in eight years as a taxi driver, I've never heard of this pub. The Kettle of Cidre, eh? Still learning, still learning."

"You'll get better when you start working back on Earth, instead of away on the moon," Ted jibed.

"That's it! You can walk home in a drunken stupor, *sir*, and I hope the steamrollers have mercy on your soul!"

"So, I'll see you in two hours?"

"Yeah, likely."

Both men laughed. *Familiarity doesn't always breed*

contempt, Ted thought; *sometimes it leads to new friendships.*

Ted was surprised that Mickey Boy – or "The Main Mouse", as he sometimes now called him – hadn't heard of The Kettle of Cidre. It was locally renowned for its thatched roof, and for dating back to the mid-eighteenth century; it was one of the oldest inns in England. In the summertime, the odd well-informed tourist even visited it as a "ye olde pub", with genuine "ye olde" heritage. The owners certainly milked it.

It had the old, latticed lead windows. Tall, carefully cultivated displays of climbing roses, supported by finely structured trellises, contrasted in brilliant sovereign reds against the perfectly maintained white walls, when in season. Even now, on this dark winter evening, with small nightlamps at the entrance and built into the eaves of the thatch, there was a warm, welcoming feel to this public house. Last time Ted had been here with Lucy and the kids, they'd had a lovely afternoon, and enjoyed a traditional cream tea, with crustless sandwiches, petit fours, clotted cream and jam scones, with tea and coffee.

Ted's latent memory brought forth those pleasing memories, of almost two and a half years earlier. Now, a much grimmer business was at hand, as Ted walked slowly through the well-kept grounds. It didn't taint his happy memories here; those memories of his family without discord actually strengthened his resolve.

As Ted searched the wood-partitioned sections of the main lounge for Jonathan, although there were only half a dozen patrons, he could feel all eyes upon him as he wandered around, anxious and mildly suspicious of being let down. "Are you okay there, sir?" came the inevitable enquiry from the bar lady.

"Yes, I'm meeting someone here – that's why I may appear to be rooting around a little bit. Could I have a pint of lager, please?" Ted asked, to placate her. Then, he studied his wristwatch and realized that he was still fifteen minutes early.

Ted sat in an alcove and tried to relax a little. He ran an index finger through the cold condensation on the side of the tall glass. It soothed him a little to draw a random line through the misty beads, revealing the mildly fizzing amber fluid beneath, beckoning him to lift the glass and sip that rich, refreshing beverage. *Only sips,* his mind interjected; *only sips until Jonathan arrives.* He wanted to give the impression of being calm and relaxed; drinking too much of his pint could belie this image. The soothing sips helped to calm him.

His eyes took in the aesthetically pleasing reproduction paintings on the walls; a Gainsborough and Canaletto style ran through them. In one, a gentleman and a lady stood proudly next to what must have been one of the biggest bulls in the world! And this would have been without the aid of steroids, Ted marvelled. Another painting, opposite the first, proposed a counter-boast, as an even more finely dressed couple accompanied a huge sheep, and the impression of a large flock of the equally sized ovines in an expansive field behind them. The third painting visible from the alcove was of a rural estate, centred by a grand mansion, perhaps two-hundred feet in length. An elongated, landscaped lake ran alongside it, double-lined with perfectly clipped and shaped trees.

"Hi, there, Mr. Fry."

Ted's absorption with the eighteenth century was brought to an end, by the voice he had been hoping to hear since first sitting down... only seven minutes ago.

"Hello, Jonathan. Here, have a seat." He noticed that Jonathan already had a pint in his hand. "You know, you can call me Ted. I'd prefer it."

"Thanks. Yeah, of course." A slightly awkward Jonathan sat opposite Ted, looking around for a few moments as he did so.

"Where are you working now?" asked Ted.

"I got a job in the city, in another bar owned by the same group. No soft-play this time, thank God! It's a wine bar called Les Vert, because it's near Queen Mary's Park," Jonathan explained.

"That sounds much better, really," Ted said.

"I'm enjoying it, and luckily I recently got a car, so it's only a twenty-minute journey to the northwest side of town," explained Jonathan.

"Do you feel comfortable talking about what happened in more detail now?" Ted asked.

"Yes, I really want to talk to you about it. I'm anxious and concerned. That soft-play needs closing down, and that area should only be used for storage, or something."

"What?" Ted spluttered a little on his lager. "Have things been that bad?"

"Well, when I spoke to you on that Thursday Toby had been acting strangely, and got upset, I wasn't able to tell you everything, because it involved other customers' children. Now that I don't work there, and the way they treated me in Cilchester, I'm quite happy to tell you about it. My only condition is that you promise not to approach the company after what I tell you," Jonathan implored Ted.

"Of course not," pledged Ted. "I'm just happy you've agreed to talk to me about it at all; it means so much to me."

Jonathan looked very concerned now. "I hope telling you is for the best, Mr.... erm, Ted.

"Well, here goes. What happened to Toby manifested itself in one child *every single* Thursday evening, within a minute or two of the same time: ten past seven."

Ted's face instantly blanched. His mouth formed a semi grimace and his eyes stared, suddenly almost doll-like, at the man delivering this shockwave. After a few seconds, his head and then his torso retreated back in his chair, until he almost became part of the alcove itself, instinctively moving away, as far as he physically could, from this threat; this verbal devastation. He felt pain in his knuckles and realized that he was gripping the frame of the chair, as if he were about to be swept away to oblivion, should he dare let go.

Jonathan's mouth gaped open at Ted's reaction. He felt tension in his scalp and a throbbing in his temples; a wave of guilt ran through him, until his throat and chest tightened. An increase in water hazed his eyes for a few seconds, then he felt mild pain in his stomach, as it reacted with an acidic release. *I've bollocked this up,* he thought, with a painfully dry attempt to gulp his Adam's apple.

They sat like this for almost thirty seconds, Jonathan staring helplessly at Ted, and Ted seeing very little but a blur at first. Nothing else could be said, until Ted recovered and consented. Jonathan's sensitivity served him well for such a young man, contrary to how he currently felt about himself.

Toward the end of these inert seconds, Ted felt basic motor thoughts returning. He released the chair from its death grip, as much through pain as through rational thinking. His immediate surroundings started to come back into focus. First to return was the form of a big, black bull, then detail of its formidable ivory horns, slightly belligerent eyes and incumbent human owners. Ted's mild long-sightedness meant that a large blur persisted in the foreground. Then he saw long, black, wiry hair, the dark goatee beard of an American Civil War Union soldier, and reasoning fired on his shocked cerebral tissue. These things were familiar and Earthly to him.

Before him, kind, very concerned eyes stared out of a face now returning to focus. Eyes now saddened and filled with humility.

"Pheeewww! What... what, actually... Just give me a moment, please," Ted twittered.

Jonathan was much more composed than Ted at this stage, perhaps not surprisingly. "Ted? Can I just go and get you a drink of water?"

Ted nodded.

Jonathan noted, with immeasurable relief, that some animation had returned to Ted's eyes. He felt able, now a few minutes on from his pistol shot, to briefly leave Ted. He swiftly returned with two glasses of iced, lemon-tinted water, from the decanter at the end of the bar. Jonathan looked gingerly at Ted, as he returned to their quiet corner. He placed a glass of water before Ted as a recommendation, then drank his own in short order, feeling instant relief against the niggling acid in his stomach. He then looked up.

"I need something a bit stronger than that," Ted self-prescribed.

Jonathan saw the return of near normality to Ted's demeanour – at least, as far as he could judge this man he hardly knew, this genuinely concerned father. Relief flowed through his body and limbs, as he realized he hadn't caused Ted any permanent damage.

"Ignore me," Ted continued, "I may just need to down a couple of pints quickly, to fortify me." He suddenly decided to gulp the water down, to reduce the symptoms of the shock.

"I'll go and get us both another pint," he volunteered. "Do you want the same again?"

Jonathan did want the same again. He needed the same medicine as his older counterpart.

Ted returned with two fresh pints of lager, under the gaze of a reserved, but nevertheless concerned barmaid, who noticed his sudden pallid and dishevelled appearance in the last fifteen minutes, after only one pint. *We don't want any more problems with drugs in this respectable establishment,* she thought to herself.

Ted presented their liquid courage and called upon new

inner resolve. "How are you for time, mate?" he queried.

"I'm in no hurry at all, Ted. I live a four-minute walk from here, in the white cottages."

"It's a really nice area," Ted admired. "I should bring my wife and kids up here more often – maybe a project for next summer."

"I take it you're in no hurry to take the kids back to The Newley?" Jonathan guessed.

"Err... there's no fear of that, mate!" Ted said, emphatically.

"It is really nice around here," Jonathan agreed, nodding several times, "except in heavy rain or snow; that T-junction becomes impassable really easily. There are quite a few power cuts, too. That generator survived the Blitz, I reckon. But, yeah, it's really nice and peaceful, but not far from the town and city."

Ted smiled, for the first time in several minutes. "I think I'm ready to hear more now."

"Are you sure?" Jonathan asked, with wide eyes. "To be honest, that is the only real shock, I think."

"Yes, please tell me more. If there are more shocks, then I need to hear them. That's what we are here for, after all," Ted said.

So, Jonathan launched straight back in once more, satisfied that Ted was ready:

"When Toby became distressed that night, I was unable to tell you that it had happened twice before on my shifts. When I looked in the register, I discovered that it hadn't only happened on my watches, but five times already; it was occurring every single Thursday, with children booking in at virtually the same time: 7:10 to 7:12."

No questions were yet forthcoming from Ted, so Jonathan continued: "And so it went on, for the full twelve weeks that I worked there; it happened six times to me, four times to my colleague and twice to the assistant manager. In fact, I believe —"

"Just a second, Jonathan," Ted had finally recovered his skills of analysis and enquiry, "how do you know what happened when you weren't on duty?"

Jonathan smiled, somewhat nervously. "Well, I was just working up to that. I worked it out by checking the register. Toby signed his name in... not the way you would expect a six-year-old to do, but how you would expect an adult to – an adult who writes in calligraphy."

Ted gawped at his informant. "No shit!" he both questioned and exclaimed in a single outburst. "Are you sure it wasn't an adult, who signed for their child on the wrong line?" Ted admitted that his reasoning was clumsy, after the shock he had just received.

Jonathan's lower teeth rose up, until they made contact with his upper lip, which they scraped against several times, rapidly. Coarse, prickly whiskers defended their southerly neighbour by irritating, scratching at the gums of their assailant. Having chastised himself thus, he released the information in a torrent of boarded-up secrets:

"*'Tobias Edward Fry, esquire'*, in the most eloquent writing; a single entry, so it couldn't be copied by anyone else." He paused, then told more – he had to, even though he already felt that he was pricking a good father with one needle after another. He felt more awful than he had done for many years – probably since he went along with bullies at school, to avoid their wrath. "Every child – all twelve – had signed their full names, in this antiquated, pristine writing! Then, each one had a strange solo experience very similar to Toby's."

Ted listened intently. He found that the young man's intense, very concerned and, most importantly, very sincere demeanour suggested strongly that he was being truthful. He believed that something was afoot.

"Can you think of any logical explanation for all of this?" Ted probed, his face now fully expressive, eyes bright and brow furled in deep thought.

"I've tried to. Really, unless this is one of the most elaborate hoaxes of all time, there is no explanation. I made enquiries with the management. The assistant manager trivialized her own experiences, saying that the children were just a bit odd; she wanted to brush it all under the carpet. So, I went above her head, by discussing it with one of the partners when he visited."

"I'm guessing here that none of the fuss was good for business, especially a new promotional venture, as the takeover has been?" predicted Ted.

"You are a wise man, Mr. Fry," Jonathan marvelled. "You've dealt with similar people? Of course you will have done..."

"Well, every business is pretty much the same, Jonathan; money, success or both are the only things that really count to most managers. They are usually people who have ideals about their line of work, and ambition. Where I work, that takes the form of meeting targets and objectives. It's just the way the world is now; some of it is for the better, some isn't."

"It doesn't sound great," Jonathan fretted.

"Maybe I'm being one-sided. I was the manager of a nursing home for five years. I really enjoyed getting my home the way I wanted it to be: raising staff morale, sharpening practice and standards of care. It's a hard and quite lonely role, apart from the few pats on the back, here and there. You are weighed down by red tape, and some of the things you are held responsible for are beyond your control – budget is the biggest one of all. Anyhoo… it's not something I want to go on about tonight; we could be here until closing time."

"Well, I find it quite interesting," Jonathan admitted. "And I'm sorry to keep calling you Mr. Fry; it's because you are more experienced and wiser than me."

Ted laughed. "Am I? I'm not so sure about the 'wiser' bit. I've just had more experience at shit-shovelling than you."

"You're being modest, Ted," said an astute Jonathan; "you are an experienced nurse, manager and father."

"I thank you for that, kind sir," said Ted, "but I have to say that you never stop learning or making mistakes. Take this soft-play business, it's making me feel helpless, sometimes inadequate even, as a father."

Jonathan took a thoughtful gulp from his warming pint. His lip curled a little in disapproval, which didn't go unnoticed by Ted.

"It's too warm in here. Our pints are not staying cold for long, are they?"

"Nah," Jonathan shook his head, "that's like a London beer!"

"I tell you what," Ted suggested, "let's gulp this one down for courage, then I'll get us another and we can ease up a bit as we talk. We need to get to the bottom of this business. Okay?"

"That sounds like a plan," grinned Jonathan. He was enjoying elements of this conversation now. Despite the initial shock he had delivered to Ted, talking with an older man as an equal was a rewarding experience. His mother was an intelligent woman but, sadly, he could not say the same of his father, for what little he saw of him. He was pleased that Ted wasn't aware of the nickname he was still known as, by some of his peers and colleagues.

I like being Jonathan, not "Tab". Sometimes he was even "Tab the Scab", to those who disliked him or felt superior. Tab had been really irresponsible, always borrowing money or asking for credit. "Can you put it on my tab?" he would say, frequently. He lost early jobs quite often, lying in, turning up mid-shift or just not bothering to give notice. He wasn't a bad youth; he had always been amiable enough, but he had just lacked purpose, direction and the guidance and support of a good role model. Jonathan, unlike Tab, was responsible, thoughtful and kind. And now he had Becka to think about and focus on. He had been with her almost two years – his longest relationship ever.

Thinking now of his lovely Becka Bumps, his smiling eyes looked up to see the welcome return of Mr. Fry, equipped with two more pints, peanuts and crisps.

"Oh, top one! This should keep us going. What else do you want to discuss?" Jonathan said, hoping now that they might be able to make some sense of all of this stuff, between the two of them.

"We are clearly dealing with the paranormal, as I think we both well know," claimed Ted, "so all we can really do is discuss what we both know, and arm ourselves with knowledge for the future."

"Arm ourselves for the future?" echoed Jonathan, in alarm. "Sounds like we're going to war."

Ted shook his head; "Not in any physical sense. I mean that we will be prepared for any future events involving the spirits and other phenomena."

"That makes some sort of sense, I suppose. It's all we can really do," a now slightly bemused Jonathan concurred.

"You have told me a lot so far, Jonathan. Now I will give you a breather and tell you about Toby. Toby is a very special little boy to me and Lucy – to his big sister, too, when she will admit it. I know all parents say the same thing about their children, but the qualifier for us is that he was born nine weeks early."

Jonathan's expression changed from interest to concern at this news. Ted saw the transformation and reassured him:

"Oh, don't worry about that; he seemed none the worse for

it, though always slightly small for his developmental markers, as he still is today, aged almost seven. Then, when he was about four, he started to manifest traits which were of concern. We noticed that he was more interested in the company of adults than he was in other children; he also liked to play with imaginary friends. He could get fixated on a certain theme, subject or even, perhaps more disturbingly, with a single item."

"Does he have autism?" Jonathan asked, running his hand through his hair, as he lowered his head.

Ted placed his hands flat on the table, and spread his fingers, in an attempt to reduce his feelings of tension. The fingertips chose their ground carefully, to avoid the wet rings, where he had forgotten to put his pints back down on the beermat. "He has mild autistic traits," Ted revealed, "but that can hardly begin to explain his behaviour at the ball park. He also told us things that I know to have happened at the old hospital, many generations ago."

Jonathan bolted to attention, almost as if a button had been pressed and given his body an automatic command. He stared intensely, waiting eagerly to hear more. Ted noted his reaction and elected to continue. It had to be done, but by disclosing a lot about his own son, he was, of course, now placing full faith in Jonathan. It was quite a gamble, about which Lucy still knew nothing, yet instinct told him that it was right to give him this information; he seemed fully trustworthy.

Looking at Jonathan now with earnest conviction, Ted continued: "Toby told me that the boy was in 'fancy-dress costume' from the Victorian period. He said that his imaginary friend was there, at The Newley Arms, because he had been very poorly, and that he was going back up to the hospital on the hill, to be back with his mum." He paused for a few seconds, so that Jonathan could have a chance to hopefully take it all in.

Jonathan appeared very tense and one hundred per cent focused, yet perhaps not as overawed by all of this new information as Ted might have been expecting. A new thought now flashed through Ted's mind: Jonathan may well know a lot about some of the other children. *He must do,* Ted reasoned, *for why else would he seem so unsurprised by what I'm telling him?* A new impulse drove Ted to enquire about this now.

"Does any of this match up to what you have experienced or heard about, Jonathan?"

Jonathan scratched his head, then his ear. He was stalling, thinking carefully before he replied, observing a touch of tension in Ted's wrinkling brow and angled eyebrows. Ted also now sat forward in his chair again, having failed in his attempts to relax. His hands were clasped before him, like the ram of an ancient Greek warship. Reading into this tension, Jonathan spoke more cautiously this time, especially after Ted's initial reaction, some twenty minutes ago. Ted had now surrendered control. He felt impotent, in dread of what he was about to be told. He expected to hear about experiences similar to Toby's, but he feared the tales to come, all the same.

"Please, just give me one moment, Mr. Fry." Jonathan glanced very slowly around him, and his right hand wandered up to his chin. A thumb gently protruded and a finely honed nail rubbed at the strong, red-brown whiskers of his beard. Ted, more or less of the generation before Jonathan's, tried to understand why young men wanted to dye long hair in a stark contrasting colour to their eyebrows and whiskers. Even above the background noise and conversations in the pub, Ted could hear Jonathan's thumbnail running through the bristle, like a plectrum vamping through guitar strings. Ted was almost as uptight as a member of the crowd awaiting the main singer, as the band vamped the artist onto the stage. Finally, Jonathan re-entered the arena.

"There was very little difference between the experiences of the six children I supervised. And Jade told me of similar events involving her four 'Thursday kids', as me and her started to call them. The floor manager pretended that nothing had happened with her two, except that two children had misbehaved and that their behaviour was caused by unruly, inattentive parents. That's typical of her: a blockheaded outlook on everything."

"Jonathan," Ted could see lined paper in a Perspex portfolio, now creeping closer and closer to the young man, "have you written all of this down?"

"No!" Jonathan looked up, furtively. "Just a few reminders, in case I was too nervous when I met you. To be honest, I am quite freaked out now, so I'm looking at my notes."

The A4-sized file Jonathan had brought in with him had a front sheet full of notes, figures and quotes. Ted had assumed that it was just paperwork, which Jonathan must have brought with him from work.

"Jonathan, that's brilliant! And very thorough. Would you be prepared to let me have a copy of them?" requested Ted.

The question brought a sudden wave of reservation down, like the steep, vertical torrent of a waterfall, with Ted on the opposite side of the wall of water from Jonathan. Jonathan's self-confidence also took a dent. *I haven't been able to handle this as well as I thought I could,* he reflected; *I'm a little bit out of my depth here. Shit! I'm a lot out of my depth! I'm chest-high in shit!*

"Oh, man," he mumbled, in exasperation, "I can't cope,

· Mr.... I mean, I'm finding this hard, Ted. I'm fucking this up!" He felt instant shame and a loss of credibility as he swore. His head retreated downward, almost level with the table. *This is a bad scene,* he thought in despair.

"Jonathan," Ted knew what was happening – in the immediate situation, at least, "we can work through this together. I feel overwhelmed, too. Can we look at your records together?"

Silence prevailed, as the tortoise-like head still receded in self-defence.

"I know I haven't the right to copy them; I've overstepped the mark there." Ted peered down, cautiously and slowly, to avoid further withdrawal from his erstwhile confidante. The confidante remained sluggish, held back by confidentiality, invasion of his privacy and a general lack of confidence.

"Yes, that seems a good compromise," he suddenly said, pushing himself out of this brief wave of inertia. It felt as if it took all of his remaining energy to do so. "There aren't any names on this summary sheet. I'll read the notes to you."

"Okay," agreed Ted, readily. He was delighted and relieved to see Jonathan rallying, when he thought everything was suddenly drying up. He saw a little blue thumbs-up sign before his eyes. "Are you happy to go through each, one at a time, so that we can discuss them thoroughly?"

A slight but positive nod of the head confirmed that they were back in business.

"Here's the first week. At 19:12, Master X came to the soft-play area. He played with three other children for about ten minutes, running around like mad, like any other five-year-old would. Then, he sidled off to play alone, as the other three continued playing together, although they were starting to tire now. I remember he was saying: 'This is not a hospital, it's a fun place,' as he threw balls at an imaginary person. He also tried to stick soft-play balls up his nose. I didn't interfere, because it clearly isn't possible to harm yourself in that way; the balls have been carefully designed to be entirely harmless, unless the attendant stands by and lets a kid chew one for ten minutes, and five- to seven-year-olds' teeth aren't that efficient. The freaky thing was, though, that he looked as if he was copying what his imaginary playmate was doing, or was being told to do it. Pretty far out! I thought I was losing it – until it started to happen every Thursday! Then the lad got annoyed, shouting and saying things like: 'You'd better stay and play here, not go to that stupid hospital!' Whereas Toby had got upset, Lia— this other boy just got angry and frustrated. So, I took him back to his parents."

Jonathan stopped at this point, tired of hearing his own voice, with his first pen picture complete. So, Ted took up the torch.

As his energy also flagged, he momentarily felt eyes upon him, above him. Was someone laughing at them, taking the piss at their expense? He felt a surge of anger. Then, as his head reached almost full trajectory, he realized that it was the proud owners of the fatted bull who were mocking him! He had studied that painting just an hour before, and didn't then take in the couple's look of disdainful amusement, but it was definitely there now. *The rich of the past diss us just the same as the rich of the present!* he inwardly laughed.

Then, he spoke: "That is very similar to what happened to Toby, isn't it? Did he see anyone in old-fashioned clothes?"

"He never said anything to me… But, then again, neither did Toby," replied Jonathan.

Ted's lightbulb switched on; "That's right. This stress is dulling my brain – probably the beer, too. Of course, he told me and Lucy later! The hospital link and the type of mimicking solo play are the same."

Ted glanced at his watch. *We still have well over an hour left,* he comforted himself. Plenty of time for this revealing conversation to shed some light on these seemingly paranormal events.

Jonathan was starting to feel better, though he had now gone all day without any weed! He decided to leave almost all of the analysis to Ted now. "Shall I tell you about the girl the next Thursday I was on? That's the week before Toby."

"Oh, definitely, please," Ted implored him.

The next story Jonathan recounted was almost identical; the imaginary companion was again male and said, almost word perfectly, the same thing. They decided to examine Jade's four accounts. Despite her slightly different way of reporting and wording from that of "Jonny", they were again almost identical in content! This seemed almost impossible. Even young children's behaviour normally contains a lot of varied detail, Ted knew.

Determined to stay in control and continue to analyze, Ted drew upon knowledge of his research from nurse training, and from when he did A-level Economics at sixth-form level. All of the variables – age, gender, the member of staff involved – made no difference to the essential events which occurred each time: the convalescent Victorian boy, with "magic" abilities, longing to get back to his mum at the community hospital. He befriended each child, then...

Ted suddenly filled up with tears. His stomach retched and he felt acrid burning in his throat. Why did he have to witness this suffering? The boy only wanted to be with his mum! What the fuck was wrong with that?

Come on, man, buck up! You have just been reassuring

Jonathan; now look at you! Right, carry on...

He befriended each child, then played with them for a while. Then, he had to – or chose to – leave them. The only variable outcome was either grief or anger for the children, and that could be based on a difference in personality, or the mood they were in at the time.

Now it was Jonathan who looked at Ted with empathy. "This is upsetting both of us; I can see how worried you are about it. If I had a child who had an experience like that, I think I would crack up."

Ted again appreciated his thoughtfulness.

Time was ticking by now. Mike would be waiting outside for Ted in about fifteen minutes. The two men had talked intensely, sharing descriptions and discussions of all of the twelve known Thursday kids. There were probably more of them since Jonathan had left.

"Shall I sum up?" Ted suggested. "We need to draw a conclusion to all we've discussed, even if there really is no satisfactory answer to all of this."

Jonathan gritted his teeth, starting to fade after four pints of lager in less than two hours. His teeth relaxed, to allow the lips to form a protruding "O" shape. A long, low whistling sound was released, before the lips drew back and merged into the beard once more. "I think there is no real conclusion, Mr. Fry.

What sense can we make of this in our world? It can never fit in."

Ted frowned in thought and narrowed his eyes. "The spiritual is in some way interacting with the physical, with our world and with our children. Let's just try, although I agree that there may be a limit to what we can actually do about it."

Jonathan gave a resigned nod. He had tried to get the soft-play area closed, but failed. He was tired now. *Home time, spliff time, bedtime. Sweet! Then my lovely lass is coming over in the morning.*

"Okay, mate," said the more enduring though also fatigued Ted, "almost home time." Sore, recently tearful eyes helped to remind him of this long day. He continued: "All of the children were alone when they saw the boy. They all seem to have seen the same boy, although Toby told me that he could change his appearance – so there's one open end. All visited on Thursday evenings at around ten past seven. All of them signed the book with eloquent writing and in their full names —"

"Oh, something important I forgot about the writing," said Jonathan: "it all looked identical. I was accused, along with Jade, of doing it as a hoax, to cause trouble."

"Erm... what about the times when the manager was supervising?" Ted queried.

"You mean the two entries blanked out carefully with high-quality liquid paper, then forged by the manager and someone else?" Jonathan became angered, for the first time in this meeting.

"Right, I'm going to go down there one Thursday – in fact, this Thursday, although Lucy might object," resolved Ted. "Don't worry, I won't divulge anything which connects me to you."

Jonathan looked relieved, which he indicated with a wink.

"So..." Ted battled on, "all of the children were alone, and none of them ever returned at the same time. Two other parents came to see you about what happened, in a constructive way, but they gave little away?" Ted paused now, for a response from Jonathan.

"Yeah, yeah, that sounds like a fair... Oh, hang on a minute, I've thought of a couple of things..." There followed a pause, so long it was almost comical. Ted had to push the conversation along:

"...And they would be?"

"They would be what?" frowned Jonathan. Then, his mind suddenly kicked back into action, and he smiled at his own doziness. "Oh, yeah... sorry, Ted, but I'm flagging now. The first thing different was on one occasion, two girls were initially going in together, but then the older one said she didn't fancy it because she had a bad tummy."

Ted looked on with interest, as Jonathan continued: "The other point I forgot to write in my notes was that one mum did ask me if there had been a fancy-dress party on in the pub."

"Oh, my giddy aunt!" Ted exclaimed. "That's food for thought! How old was the girl who didn't want to go in?"

"I'd say about eight... not too old. It's unusual for a kid that age to turn down soft-play. The mum of the other girl explained that her daughter had met a boy who looked like a chimney sweep from an old children's musical, the same as what Toby told you."

"That does give us another link to the children," Ted recapped. "It's a big assumption, but we can probably kind of take it as read that all of the kids saw the same Victorian boy."

Jonathan, finding his last seam of energy, anticipated Ted's conclusion in his own words: "So... The Newley Arms appears to be haunted!"

Ted laughed: "You've more or less taken the words right out of my mouth, you bugger!"

Jonathan gave a tired smile, suppressing a yawn as he did so. "Yeah. I'm still here... kinda."

"Let's call it a day," Ted advised. "We must keep in touch, though; I have your number."

"Yes, I'd like a text or two about your visit on Thursday,

please, Mr.... Ted."

Ted smiled at Jonathan's struggle with consciousness. "Thank you so much for all of your time and effort," Ted said, giving him a hearty pat on the shoulder.

They left together, again feeling the eyes of the barmaid and a few locals upon them.

"Goodnight, gents. Thank you," she shouted, with a hint of insincerity. Once the two tall figures had disappeared out of the main entrance, she turned to her potman; "I wonder what those two are up to... They seem a weird pair to me."

The potman just smiled, then turned back to his work, his eyes rolling at the ideas of the gossip-mongering barmaid. *That will keep the old crow in gossip for a fortnight,* he thought to himself.

Finale

Thursday came.

Ted had, through necessity, spilt the beans to Lucy about his investigations. She had been much more understanding than he expected, but wanted to stay on the fringes.

He therefore found himself plodding through puddles on an uninviting night, cold, nervous and alone. Destination: The Newley Arms. Where else? Ted's shoes had started to let in deep water. Cilchester lay at the base of a very deep valley, so water collected fast and furious, whenever there was heavy rain.

I won't hang around in here, he promised himself. I'll spend enough time to gather information, without raising suspicion, then scarper straight back home.

Yet, despite this resolve, even at the doorway to the pub he stopped, to read a large sign:

"WE APOLOGIZE FOR THE RECENT CLOSURE OF
OUR SOFT-PLAY AREA.
THE NEW IMPROVED AND EXTENDED SOFT-PLAY
WILL BE OPEN FROM 20th JULY"

My god, that's next Thursday! Let's hope the change of location, with a new build, will break the curse!

Ted folded his umbrella and gave it a good shake, in the external overhang of the pub's main door. He found himself already pondering, even speculating. Had the owners been forced by events to relocate the soft-play facility, after less than four months? Maybe Jonathan had more influence than he realized? Whichever way, this was a very important development.

Ted sauntered into the main bar and dining area, as casually as possible. The warm air, filled with pleasant aromas of cooking food and coffee beans, was most welcome. Despite his plan to be casual, his eyes were drawn, like two magnetized steel balls, toward the far dining area, where his family had sat on that fateful night, exactly eleven weeks ago. It looked the same in layout, yet was now quite dimly lit. Not wanting to stare into the middle ground for too long, Ted deliberately turned toward the main bar area – though it was difficult to do so.

The tiny young barmaid smiled: "Do you need a table, sir?"

"No, thanks," he smiled back, "just a pint of lager, please."

A waiter came behind the bar, to open a tab for one of the dining tables. "It's getting busy, Jade," he grumbled.

Jade! What a stroke of luck!

So, this was Jade, who shared Jonathan's weird experiences with the Thursday kids? Ted needed to hang around near the bar for a while, but he had to do so without making it too obvious – and without appearing a letch. He needed a plan to talk to her...

Ted took his inviting pint, and tried to settle down at the cubicle nearest to the bar. It sported a double, dark-red, padded seat against the small, high window, at a right angle to the bar serving area. The cubicle's open central section allowed good eavesdropping, whilst the glass and wood partition adjoining the seats and raised floor hid the patron – in this case, Ted – from the bar staff's view.

It seemed great for a couple of minutes, as Ted clearly heard all about Vera's grandbairns, what Louise bought in the clothes shops in the city yesterday, and how Monty, the golden Labrador, rolled in pig shit near the local farm. Then it rapidly dawned on Ted that this spot was all well and good for surveillance of the staff's conversations, but useless for subtly getting Jade's attention.

Ted's shoes remained uncomfortable. The dampness of the leather, combined with wet nylon socks, gave off a disagreeable "foisty" smell, as the heat started to dry them, which distracted from his beer and his concentration.

Listening to the trivial talk, he started to gulp down his pint. A higher risk strategy was bolting through his head; another bullet train arriving at the station! This newly conceived scheme demanded quick but, hopefully, not rash action. Briefly emboldened by a rapid intake of alcohol, Ted, upon hearing Jade's voice, bounded from the cubicle to the bar in two seconds. Jade caught Ted's movement from a peripheral angle, and spun around to meet it.

"Thirsty tonight, sir?" she enquired, with a pleasant smile which contradicted that any trace of sarcasm could be found in her comment, by an unknown patron.

"Yes, yes, I've had a long, stressful day. Same again, please, Miss...?"

"Jade," she replied, glancing down at her name badge, this time with a nervous smile.

"Oh! Jade!" Ted said loudly, with a deceiving mock surprise. "My neighbour was down here recently, and recommended that I should bring my family back again. She said that the soft-play attendant, Jade, was a natural with the kids. Brilliant, just brilliant!"

Jade shrank back from the counter a little, in instinctive self-defence.

Ted's anxiety and single-mindedness stopped him from reading into the poor girl's body language, as he would normally have done. "I was thinking of bringing my son back again, although he got a bit upset the last time he was here."

Jade held back, concentrating on getting Ted's next pint. This man was giving her a torrent of information, and seemingly pleasant with it, but could be possibly about to make a scene or a complaint. It was happening a lot here lately, since the takeover. *I don't need this grief: another complaint about the soft-play area!*

She created a pregnant pause, preparing herself for the worst, but no punchline came from this gentleman. He was now awaiting a response from her.

"I only covered as soft-play attendant now and then. Was I on when your son was here?" she enquired.

"No," Ted was starting to realize how farcical his behaviour was, but he had to continue lying, because of his pledge to Jonathan, "my wife said it was an older lady who was at the desk."

"Ah, yes, she's the manager," Jade revealed, with a thinly concealed, weary sigh.

"I want my boy to come back to enjoy it next time," gushed Ted. "It's so handy for us."

"Soft-play is closed at the moment, but it opens on Thursday next week, a week today," said Jade, with some formality."

"Why did they close it?" Ted probed.

"Erm... I think they wanted to make it bigger," she said.

Ted decided to leave it at that. "Okay, thanks. I'll bring him down when it opens."

"Thank you for the kind feedback." Jade's voice followed him across the main dining area, as he quickly advanced.

He went to sit down with his second pint, where he could reflect on what a prat he had been. *I must salvage something from all of this, or I might as well just take up knitting instead – that could be more frigging useful at this rate, especially with Christmas approaching!*

But Ted didn't sit down. He wandered straight toward the location where the soft-play area had been. He felt diners' eyes upon him, but he cared little.

To his amazement, when he peered nervously into the offending area, he found that it had already been completely refurbished. It had been made into a most unusually large, themed anteroom, almost one-third of the size of the rest of the pub combined. Picture lights provided the main source of illumination. The pictures featured old panoramic photos of Cilchester and its environs.

Ted's immediate attention was drawn to a fascinating collection of artefacts, on a long shelf which spanned some twenty feet of the back wall. There was an old clothes iron, with a hinged top and a wooden handle, presumably to be filled with hot water from a kettle, or perhaps hot embers and coals from the fire. *How interesting!* Next to it was a washboard, with a small laundry basin, almost like a miniature tin bath. Ted laughed; it reminded him of old comedy films and music hall acts, where things such as "Oops, where's me washboard?" would be said, in an early form of alternative comedy. At least, that was Ted's interpretation.

He then had a more sobering realization of how hard life must have been then; how labour intensive the simplest household tasks were – hence the shorter life spans, and the early-life ailments and diseases.

In the centre was a childhood theme. Old pens had been placed in inkpots, ranging from quills to the later, yet almost as primitive, nibs on sticks. A miniature blackboard, with chalks and a cloth eraser, was next in line. His eyes scanned along to a traditional teddy bear; *Ahh, my namesake,* Ted thought, happily thinking of his loving wife. And then – *Oh, no!* – a dog on wheels, which looked extraordinarily like old Penny, his Bedlington terrier back home. Ted had seen these wheeled dogs before, in books and museums, but he still couldn't help laughing at the sight of poor Penny stuck onto a wheeled trolley.

"I'm pleased my humble display amuses you."

Ted got a start from the sudden voice behind him. The

room was deserted when he had first arrived, just two minutes ago. He spun around fast, catching his knuckles on the sharp-edged frame of the wheeled terrier.

The croaky, crackly voice produced a further enquiry: "Are you okay there, sir?" The voice belonged to a very slightly built, elderly man, peering over old-fashioned, wire-framed penny spectacles. He was balding, still with dark sideburns, his age revealed by baggy eyes and loose skin on his chin, merging into a wrinkled neck. He wore nondescript, sack-like, dark clothing.

"I see I gave you a start," the man continued, almost seeming to read Ted's thoughts.

Ted nursed his painful hand, noting that the old gentleman was reading a very old broadsheet newspaper.

"Oh, it's my hobby," said the old gentleman, as he noticed that Ted was staring, puzzled by his reading material. "I've been reading the papers since 1852!" He started to chuckle, in a feint, croaking style which matched his voice.

Ted finally found his tongue: "It is a very impressive, thoughtfully presented collection. Almost a museum within a pub! Well done, Mr....?"

"Man. Mr. Man," the old fellow nodded. "Please, don't let me distract you; you have still to look at the photographs." He grinned knowingly, almost cruelly, in anticipation of events.

His voice emitted a certain persuasive quality – a knowing enlightenment, which intrigued Ted and enticed him, most strangely, to do as the gentleman invited.

As Ted turned to look at the large photo before him, he felt sticky, thickening fluid between his thumb and index finger. The skin on his knuckles was torn worse than he had at first realized, and he could smell the all too familiar, sickly sweet, iron-rich hallmark of blood. Yet, the old gentleman's words superseded the urge of self-preservation, and before going to the toilets, to clean the wound, Ted briefly looked up at the photo before him.

In the middle of Cilchester's main street stood a boy, quite alone on a bright day. He wore a dark cloth cap, a mid-Victorian-era linen blouse and baggy trousers, held in place by improvised sisal string braces. He was barefoot.

But all of these details paled into insignificance when he suddenly smiled. He smiled at Ted, in the way that the man in the T.V. had smiled, all those years ago…!

Ted suddenly felt an acrid stinging in his throat. Sickened and shocked, both physically and mentally, he turned and stumbled away. And, looking to the old man for further counsel, he faced new despair… the old man was not there!

All that lay on the table, where he had sat and talked to Ted, was a partly read, crumpled edition of today's newspaper.

Hospital Spirits

About the Author

Paul Fields majored in History at The University of Kirklees (then Huddersfield Polytechnic) from 1982- 85. After periods of self employment , Paul trained as a Registered General Nurse in 1988. He has worked in a wide range of hospital and Nursing Home settings. His greatest privelidge has been to spend so many engaging years with older persons . It is they who have provided the main inspiration for his introductory work "Hospital Spirits" . Paul is also a passionate historian , having met hundreds of world war Two veterans in his travels as a History Guide in France , Holland and Belgium. He has produced an unpublished work of war poems , featuring and dedicated to the men and women who endured World War II .

Acknowledgements

The publisher would like to thank Russell Spencer, Matt Vidler, Laura-Jayne Humphrey, Lianne Bailey-Woodward, Leonard West and Susan Woodard for their hard work and efforts in bringing this book to publication.

The author would like to thank all of the care assistants and nurses who have inspired, encouraged and sustained him in the development of this book. Special thanks also to his Wife , Bev for her measured and realistic support and for character inspiration.

Hospital Spirits

About the Publisher

L.R. Price Publications is dedicated to publishing books by unknown authors.

We use a mixture of both traditional and modern publishing options, to bring our authors' words to the wider world. We print, publish, distribute and market books in a variety of formats including paper and hardback, electronic books, digital audiobooks and online.

If you are an author interested in getting your book published, or a book retailer interested in selling our books, please contact us.

www.lrpricepublications.com

L.R. Price Publications Ltd,
27 Old Gloucester Street,
London, WC1N 3AX.
020 3051 9572
publishing@lrprice.com

Printed in Great Britain
by Amazon

79175915R00129